FIRST OF ALL

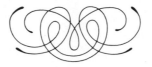

FIRST of ALL

SIGNIFICANT
———— "FIRSTS" ————
BY AMERICAN WOMEN

JOAN McCULLOUGH

Holt, Rinehart and Winston *New York*

Copyright © 1980 by Joan McCullough
All rights reserved, including the right to reproduce
this book or portions thereof in any form.
Published by Holt, Rinehart
and Winston, 383 Madison Avenue,
New York, New York 10017.
Published simultaneously in Canada by
Holt, Rinehart and Winston of Canada, Limited.

Library of Congress Cataloging in Publication Data
McCullough, Joan.
First of all.
Includes index.
1. Women in the professions—United States—Biography
2. Success. I. Title.
HQ1412.M24   305.4'0973   80-3444

ISBN Hardcover: 0-03-057644-X
ISBN Paperback: 0-03-0850941-6
First Edition

Designer: Amy Hill
Printed in the United States of America
1 3 5 7 9 10 8 6 4 2

To my grandmother,

ETHEL VIRGINIA WRIGHT,

*the first woman postmaster
of Mary Esther, Florida.*

CONTENTS

ARMED SERVICES   5

The 1ST Admitted to full rank and military status in the U.S. ARMED SERVICES • Soldier in the U.S. ARMY • Confederate ARMY officer • U.S. ARMY pension recipient • U.S. Air Force Academy CADETS • U.S. Coast Guard Academy CADETS • U.S. Merchant Marine Academy CADETS • West Point (U.S. Military Academy) CADETS • Ship CAPTAIN of a U.S. vessel • U.S. COAST GUARD officers assigned to duty aboard ships • CONGRESSIONAL MEDAL OF HONOR recipient • Navy FLIGHT SURGEONS • Two-star GENERAL • Brigadier (one-star) GENERALS • U.S. Naval Academy MIDSHIPMEN • Coast Guard PILOT • Military PILOTS to fly for the United States • Navy PILOTS

ARTS AND ENTERTAINMENT   21

The 1ST ACTRESS to win the Academy Award • Black ACTRESS to win an Academy Award • ACTRESS to win an Obie • ARCHITECT • Syndicated CARTOONIST • CLOWN in the Ringling Brothers and Barnum & Bailey Circus • CONDUCTOR on Broadway • CONDUCTOR at the Metropolitan

- Pictured on U.S. CURRENCY • Black MILLIONAIRE • PATENT HOLDER • PROSTITUTES UNION • PUBLISHER of the Declaration of Independence • STOCK EXCHANGE DIRECTOR • WORLD'S FAIR

EDUCATION 71

COLLEGE • COLLEGE PRESIDENT • NOBEL PEACE PRIZE recipient • RHODES SCHOLARS from the United States • SORORITY

POLITICS, LAW, AND LAW ENFORCEMENT 79

CABINET member • Secretary of Commerce in a U.S. CABINET • Secretary of Health, Education and Welfare in a U.S. CABINET • Secretary of Housing and Urban Development in a U.S. CABINET • CONGRESSWOMAN • Black CONGRESSWOMAN • Avowed lesbian COUNCIL MEMBER elected to a city council • COUNCIL PRESIDENT in New York City • DESIGNER of a state seal • DISTRICT ATTORNEY • GOVERNOR whose husband did not precede her in office • GOVERNOR • White INDIAN CHIEF • JUDGE in the U.S. Court of Appeals for the Second Circuit • Black federal JUDGE • JUSTICE OF THE PEACE • National LABOR UNION • LAWYER • Black LAWYER • LAWYER to present a case before the U.S. Supreme Court • Black LAWYER to present a case before the U.S. Supreme Court • Avowed lesbian LEGISLATOR • MAYOR • POLICE DETECTIVE • PRESIDENTIAL CANDIDATE • PRISONER EXECUTED for crimes against the government • PRISONER EXECUTED in the electric chair • QUEEN of American descent • SENATOR

game played at Madison Square Garden • Professional BASKETBALL league • Olympic BASKETBALL team from the United States • Six-day BICYCLE RACE • CAMP FIRE GIRLS • CANOEIST to make a solo trip down the Mississippi • CREW • DAREDEVIL to conquer Niagara Falls in a barrel • GIRL SCOUTS • President of the GIRL SCOUTS • Black president of the GIRL SCOUTS • HORSEBACK RIDER to make a coast-to-coast ride • JOCKEY to compete against men on a major U.S. flat track • JOCKEY to win at a major U.S. flat track • MARATHON runner to win in open competition against men • Unofficial Boston MARATHON competitor • "Official" Boston MARATHON competitor • Officially sanctioned Boston MARATHON finisher • MOTORCYCLISTS to ride coast to coast • MOUNTAINCLIMBER to scale Mount Rainier • MOUNTAINCLIMBERS to scale Mt. Annapurna • OLYMPIC GOLD MEDALIST • Runner to win three OLYMPIC GOLD MEDALS • PARACHUTIST to jump from an airplane • SOAP BOX DERBY CHAMPION • Professional SOFTBALL league • STEAMBOAT CAPTAIN on the Mississippi • STEAMBOAT CAPTAIN west of the Mississippi • STEAMBOAT CAPTAIN of the Delta Queen • SULLIVAN AWARD winner • SWIMMER to cross the English Channel • SWIMMER to cross the English Channel in both directions • SWIMMER to break the record for circling the island of Manhattan • UMPIRE in professional baseball • VARSITY letter winner at a military academy • Member of a male college VARSITY TEAM

LIST OF ILLUSTRATIONS

ACKNOWLEDGMENTS

For various forms of support and encouragement I am especially thankful to the following: my friends, Shirley Stoler, Katie Kelly, Marilyn Wagner and the late Sally Rand; my agent, Bobbe Siegel; Bobbi Mark and Anice Mills of Holt, Rinehart and Winston; my aunt, Bess Surette; my research assistant, Patricia Ann Summers; and my friends at 300 West 17th Street.

FIRST OF ALL

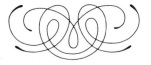

INTRODUCTION

In 1973, while researching a piece on aviation, I came upon some news clippings from 1959 that absolutely astonished me. They were accounts of a group of women pilots who had been recruited to take the same physical and psychological tests underway at that time on John Glenn, Alan Shepard, and other potential astronaut candidates. Over half the women passed the first set of tests with high marks, and the first three to complete the entire series were rated as superb candidates for space flight—yet not one of them was selected for the program. My astonishment came from the fact that I had never heard of these women before and from my realization that I would not have found out about them except by accident. There had been detailed accounts in newspaper and magazine articles and in various reports at the time; but in the years that followed, their presence had somehow been overshadowed by the ensuing glory of the men who got the jobs. From that time on, I found it difficult to hear of a woman who had run for office, or established a new sports record, or invented something, without wanting to know who, if not that woman, had done it—or tried to do it— first. Not because there was special merit attached to the fact for its own sake, but because of the perspective it lent to events that followed.

Finding out about these pioneers was not always easy, since there was no single source available as a guide for that kind of information where women were concerned. On one occasion, when comparing some encyclopedia entries about the *Mayflower*, I found a detailed description of all the Pilgrim men, including complete lists of all male passengers and male servants. There was, however, not so much as a mention of any women, except an indirect one noting that two babies had been born on board. In any case, I have in the meantime accumulated a file full of wonderfully interesting women whose lives, for the most part, were previously unknown to me. I think of Annie Edson Taylor who toppled over Niagara Falls in 1901 inside a leaky wooden barrel (the first person of either sex to do it and survive), under conditions that would make Evel Knievel hang up his helmet. And Deborah Sampson, a schoolteacher who during the Revolution was wielding a musket as a foot soldier in the Colonial Army; or Mary Katherine Goddard, up to her elbows in printer's ink at the same time, turning out first editions of the Declaration of Independence. Later, in the pioneer days of aviation, women made some of the most important contributions in that field. Georgia "Tiny" Broadwick, who made the first parachute jumps by a woman, later made the first free-fall jump while attempting to demonstrate to military brass the wisdom of equipping their pilots with parachutes. As a result, the Army placed its first order that day. Not all of these women who were "first" were so brave, nor were most of them particularly interested in achieving that distinction. Some were first by coincidence, like the brilliant astronomer Maria Mitchell, who gazed into her telescope on a fortuitous night in 1847 and discovered a new comet. And someone just happened to remember the name of a young social worker named

Amelia Earhart when a group of promoters were look-
ing around for a woman who might like to fly across
the Atlantic. Earhart, who weathered the attending
strain of pioneering better than most people and went
on to fly both oceans on her own, remarked philo-
sophically about being first that "somebody has to."
Occasionally, the rewards for being first were both
brief and bittersweet. When Berenice Gera, America's
first woman umpire called her first game in 1972, she
made a mistake, then broke down under the ridicule
that followed, and quit that same day. Her experiences,
if nothing else, are a testimonial to the difficulties
incumbent upon those who lead the way, especially
into hostile territory. Dorothy Fuldheim became the
nation's first television anchorwoman back in 1947. Her
sponsor, a beer company, at first refused to tolerate
a woman in that position. But her station stood by
her, and at the age of eighty-six, she was still on
the air, one of the nation's most respected broadcast
journalists.

Today, as our culture becomes ever more success-
oriented, those women who rise, or appear to rise,
into prominence become representatives in recorded
history. The contributions of women in general, and
society's expectations for them, tend to be perceived
from those isolated high points, which are seen independently by each generation, instead of in a con-
tinuum. Where the women on the following pages are
concerned, those who were financially successful fared
better historically, especially where accounts of first
achievements by minority women are concerned. Even
Annie Taylor would, I'm sure, not have been so quickly

forgotten after her trip over the falls had she opened a barrel factory and made a million dollars selling powder kegs.

In describing the formation of the seas, Rachel Carson observed that beginnings are apt to be shadowy. Here then, in the interest of bringing us out of the shadows and into the ocean of our own history, are some beginnings.

Joan McCullough   1979

The designer has devised a symbol, *, which will appear at the beginning of each entry as a substitution where the words "first female," "first woman," "first young woman,"—or the corresponding plural—"first women's" or simply "first" would be appropriate.*

ARMED SERVICES

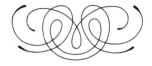

The **1ST** *admitted to full rank and military status in the U.S.* **ARMED SERVICES** were inducted during World War I. In 1915 the U.S. Navy recruited some eleven thousand women into the Naval Reserves as Yeomen (F), indicating "female." Another five hundred joined the Marine Reserves. The women ran munition factories, drove ambulances, and performed a variety of noncombat duties. They continued to serve for the duration of the war but were deactivated when it ended in 1918.

On leave from the U.S. Navy Reserve during World War I, a group of Yeomen (F) enjoy a recreational game of billiards.

A group of female inductees take the oath and are sworn in as members of the U.S. Marine Reserves during World War I.

The 1ST *Soldier in the U.S.* **ARMY** was Deborah Sampson, born in Plympton, Massachusetts, in 1760. At the age of twenty-two, Sampson, a schoolteacher, donned male attire and hiked to Boston, where she enlisted in the Continental Army under the name Robert Shurtleff. At 5-foot-8, she easily passed for a youthful male. Sworn in without question, she served for over a year in the Fourth Massachusetts Regiment of General George Webb and was commended as an outstanding soldier. Once, in a skirmish near West Point, she reputedly removed a musket ball from her own thigh with a penknife rather than risk discovery by allowing a doctor to do it. Some months later, in Pennsylvania, she contracted a high fever and lapsed into unconsciousness. In the hospital, a physician discovered that Private Shurtleff was a woman and prescribed a hasty, though honorable discharge upon her recovery. Sampson returned to Massachusetts to begin life anew, settling in the town of Sharon, some miles away from her native Plympton. Rumors of her military past soon reached the tiny community, however, making it difficult for her to find work. With few options open, she accepted an offer of marriage from Benjamin Gannett, a local farmer. The couple eventually had three children. Gannett was not successful as a farmer, and at one point Deborah presented some theatrical tours to help support the family. Dressed in her old Army uniform, she would give a short lecture about her military adventures, then dazzle the audience with a precision rifle drill. In 1792, at the urging of her friend and neighbor, Paul Revere (from whom she had been forced to borrow money), Deborah applied for veterans' benefits. The state of Massachusetts sent thirty-four pounds, plus interest to the date of her discharge, by then ten years earlier. And, after an embarrassed delay, the federal government followed suit with a monthly stipend of four dollars. Deborah died in 1827 and was buried in the Rock Ridge Cemetery in Sharon. After her death, Mr. Gannett asked for and received a widower's pension as the surviving spouse of a veteran.

The **1ST** *Confederate* **ARMY** *officer* was Sally Louisa Tompkins, who was born in Poplar Grove, Virginia, in 1833. When the Civil War began, Tompkins, a humanitarian and philanthropist, turned her Richmond home into a hospital, which she staffed and supported with her own money. Later that year for security reasons, Jefferson Davis issued an executive order closing all private hospitals, but he so respected Tompkins's work that he commissioned her a captain in the cavalry, thereby granting military sanction to her hospital. It remained open throughout the war and was credited with saving more lives than any other medical institution. The only woman known to have belonged to the Confederate Army, Captain Sally Tompkins lived to be ninety-two. She died in Richmond in 1916 and was given a military funeral.

The **1ST** *U.S.* **ARMY** *pension recipient* was Margaret "Molly" Corbin, born in Pennsylvania in 1751. During the Revolutionary War, she accompanied her husband, a cannon loader, to the battlefield at Fort Washington, New York. When the British attacked on November 16, 1776, her husband was fatally wounded. Without hesitating, Molly Corbin took his place, continuing to sponge out and reload the cannon until the battle ended. Wounded by gunfire, she was taken prisoner by the British and moved with other survivors to New York City, where she was eventually released. After serving briefly as a volunteer with a training and recruitment unit, she withdrew because of her injuries and sought treatment at West Point. Army officials knew of the Fort Washington heroine and began appeals to the government for assistance on her behalf. Pennsylvania responded with a thirty-dollar grant, and in July 1779, Congress approved her military pension, including all the benefits normally extended to a Revolutionary War veteran. She was permitted to draw rations from the military stores and was treated at the military hospital. She never fully recovered from her wounds, however, and entirely lost the use of one arm. She died in 1800 and is buried at the West Point cemetery.

The 1ST *U.S. Air Force Academy* **CADETS** reported for training at Colorado Springs, Colorado, on June 28, 1976. There were 157 women in the academy's 1,593-member freshman class of 1980. (Over 1,200 women had applied.) To assist in training, the academy supplemented the staff with female officers from the regular Air Force for the first year; and as the new women cadets attained upperclass status, they assumed responsibility for training underclass cadets. In May of 1980, 98 out of the original 157 women graduated.

The 1ST *U.S. Coast Guard Academy* **CADETS** were offered appointments on February 4, 1976. They were Kathryn Lis of Bristol, Connecticut, Susan Kollmeyer of Groton, Connecticut, and Cynthia Snead of Melbourne, Florida, who were in the top 1 percent of the ten thousand male and female applicants competing to enter the class of 1980. Within the next few months, thirty-five other women were selected. Unlike the other service academies, the Coast Guard Academy, located at New London, Connecticut, bases its admissions solely on nationwide competition, with no congressional appointments or geographical quotas.

U.S. Merchant Marine Academy **CADETS** reported to the academy at Kings Point, New York, in July 1974. It was the first time in the nation's history that women were admitted to one of the five service academies. On June 26, 1978, eight of the original fifteen graduated with B.S. degrees, deck or engineering licenses to work aboard U.S. Merchant Marine vessels, and commissions in the U.S. Naval Reserve. They were: Della Anholt, 23, of Portland, Oregon; Ivy Barton, 24, of New Castle, Delaware; Rochon Greene, 22, of Dallas, Texas; Kathy Metcalf, 23, of Dover, Delaware; Meredith Neizer, 22, of Smyrna, Delaware; Teresa Olsen, 21, of Pensacola, Florida; Nancy Wagner, 23, of Woodcliff Lake, New Jersey; and Frances Yates, 21, of Seattle, Washington.

West Point (U.S. Military Academy) **CADETS** joined "the long gray line" in 1976. Out of the 867 women who applied, 119 passed the academic, physical, and medical standards necessary to become members of the entering class of 1980. Academic requirements were identical to those for males, medical requirements were the same as for women commissioned into the regular Army, and physical requirements were adjusted slightly to allow for certain physiological differences such as weight, height, and strength between average males and females. Sixty-one of the original 119 who entered graduated in the spring of 1980.

The **1ST** *ship* **CAPTAIN** *of a U.S. vessel* was Coast Guard Lieutenant jg. Beverly Kelley, who was appointed commander of the ninety-five-foot cutter *Cape Newagen* in April 1979. With a home port of Maalea, Maui, Hawaii, Captain Kelley's ship was responsible for search and rescue missions, law enforcement, antipollution enforcement, and boating safety in nearby Pacific waters. Lieutenant Kelley, a native of Miami, Florida, graduated from the Coast Guard Officer Candidate School in Yorktown, Virginia, on June 3, 1976.

The **1ST** *U.S.* **COAST GUARD** *officers assigned to duty aboard ships* were Ensign Terry Irene Burton, 26, and Ensign Deborah Gail Nelson, 24, both of whom graduated from the Coast Guard Officer Candidate School in Yorktown, Virginia, on June 7, 1979. Nelson, a native of Frostburg, Maryland, reported immediately to the Coast Guard cutter *Gallatin* at Governors Island, New York, and Burton, from La Habra, California, went to the cutter *Morgenthau*.

1ST CONGRESSIONAL MEDAL OF HONOR *recipient* was Dr. Mary Edwards Walker, a Civil War surgeon. Born in Oswego, New York, in 1832, she graduated from Syracuse Medical College in 1855. An early reformer, she scorned traditional female attire as impractical, and at her wedding that year to Albert Miller, a fellow medical student, she appeared in trousers. She further defied convention by eliminating the vows to honor or obey him and by refusing to take his name. (They were ultimately divorced.) At the outbreak of the war Dr. Walker went to Washington, hoping to join the medical corps, but she was refused admission because of her sex. Doctors were badly needed, however, so she was allowed to treat the wounded in hospitals and on the battlefield, but only as an unpaid volunteer. Finally, after two years, she was given a commission and a salary. Dr. Walker angered many soldiers by boldly wearing an Army uniform complete with gold-striped trousers and the green sash that signified medical status. Her devotion and bravery were unquestioned, however. In 1865 she was captured and imprisoned for many months and was finally released in exchange for a Confederate officer. When the war ended, General Sherman himself recommended her for the Medal of Honor, and President Andrew Johnson presented it to her on November 11, 1865. She was extremely proud of the decoration and wore it often, especially when speaking in public about women's suffrage or dress reform, her two favorite causes. Her unconventional behavior continued to make her the object of much ridicule, however, and she found it increasingly difficult to earn a living. By 1887 she was reduced to appearing in sideshows, and a few years later she moved back to Oswego. On June 3, 1917, an Army review board revoked her award, alleging that she had not deserved it and that her military status had been unclear. Informed of their demands for its return, she staunchly refused to give up the medal. She wore it until she died three years later at the age of eighty-seven. Through the efforts of a grandniece and members of Congress, it was formally restored to her on June 10, 1977.

Battlefield surgeon Dr. Mary Edwards Walker wears the Congressional Medal of Honor presented to her in 1865 for heroic service during the Civil War. THE SMITHSONIAN INSTITUTION

The 1ST *Navy* **FLIGHT SURGEONS** were Lieutenants Victoria M. Voge and Jane D. McWilliams, who graduated from the Navy's flight surgeon training program at the Naval Aerospace Medical Institute in Pensacola, Florida, on December 20, 1973.

Both ranked in the top half of their class and were the first women to be graduated from the program in its fifty-one-year history.

In 1973, Brigadier General Jeanne Holm of the U.S. Air Force was awarded her second star, making her the nation's first major general.

The 1ST two-star **GENERAL** was Jeanne M. Holm, Director of Women in the Air Force, who had been one of the first women to achieve the rank of brigadier general. Holm was born in Portland, Oregon, and was a professional silversmith before enlisting in the Army in 1942. After World War II she left active duty but was recalled in 1949 and transferred to the Air Force. She served as Director of Women beginning in 1965 and is credited with effecting a number of changes for Air Force women. She modernized uniforms, updated policies affecting women, and expanded assignment and job opportunities, all of which resulted in a doubling of WAF strength under her leadership. Her second star was pinned on in June 1973. General Holm retired in 1975.

The **1ST** *brigadier (one-star)* **GENERALS** *in the U.S. Armed Services* achieved the rank in 1970. They were Colonel Mildred C. Bailey, Director of the Women's Army Corps; Colonel Jeanne M. Holm, Director of Women in the Air Force; Colonel Anna M. Hayes, retired Chief of the Army Nurses Corps; Colonel Lillian Dunlap, Chief of the Army Nurses Corps; and Colonel Elizabeth P. Hoisington, retired Director of the Women's Army Corps. In 1972, Captain Arlene Duerk of the Navy Nurse Corps became the first woman to achieve the rank of Admiral in all of the world's navies.

The **1ST** *U.S. Naval Academy* **MIDSHIPMEN** reported to Annapolis, Maryland, in July 1976. The eighty-one women faced the same general admissions standards as male applicants, except for minor adjustments in the physical requirements. In the summer of 1979, for the first time in academy history, the first female seniors were assigned training duty in the fleet aboard ships. Upon graduation in 1980, the fifty-five women who survived the course received B.S. degrees and commissions in the Navy or Marine Corps.

The 1ST *Coast Guard* **PILOT** was Janna Lambine, one of the first women admitted to the previously all-male U.S. Coast Guard Officer Candidate School in Yorktown, Virginia. While there, she applied and was accepted for flight training at the Naval Air Station in Pensacola, Florida. On March 4, 1977, she received her wings and went to work flying helicopters for the Coast Guard.

The 1ST *military* **PILOTS** *to fly for the United States* were the WASPs (Women's Air Force Service Pilots) of World War II. In 1941 armed forces leaders feared a shortage of combat pilots and followed a suggestion by Jacqueline Cochran (see *first female*

Four World War II WASP pilots, parachutes in hand, head for the hangars at a Texas airfield after a long day of flying B–17s. NATIONAL AIR AND SPACE MUSEUM, SMITHSONIAN INSTITUTION

PILOT to break the sound barrier, page 57) and others that women pilots be utilized for noncombat missions. Some 25,000 applications came in from women pilots who wanted to join, out of which 1,875 were accepted. Sent to Houston and then to Avenger Field in Sweetwater, Texas, 1,100 survived the rugged training that turned them into military pilots. Then they went to work piloting for navigators and bombardiers in training, performing searchlight and tracking missions, and towing targets while male combat pilots shot at them with live ammunition. The women flew every kind of plane the military owned or would develop during the war, including fighter planes, (called "pursuits") bombers, drones, and the military's first jets. But male civilian contract pilots, whose lucrative jobs they had been filling for a fraction of the cost, complained to Congress, and in 1944 the WASPs were deactivated. Forming the Order of Finfinella, named after the female gremlin who had been their wartime mascot, the WASPs appealed for veterans' benefits but were denied them until 1978. It was only then that Congress admitted that the 850 surviving WASPs were entitled to medical and other benefits routinely granted to veterans.

The **1ST** *Navy* **PILOTS** began their training on March 2, 1973, at Pensacola, Florida. They were Lieutenant jg. Judith Neuffer of Worcester, Massachusetts; Lieutenant jg. Barbara Allen Rainey of Bethesda, Maryland; Ensign Jane Skiles Odea of

Ames, Iowa; Ana Marie Fuqua of McLean, Virginia; Joellen Drag of Castro Valley, California; and Rosemary Conatser of San Diego, California. Three of the women were already in the Navy, and three were recruited from civilian life. Two other qualified women were also selected for the program but did not complete the course. They were Ensign Kathleen McNary and civilian Joanne Hellman. The graduates received their Navy wings on February 18, 1975.

Lieutenant Judith Neuffer was among the first female graduates of the Navy's flight training program. Her first assignment was flying into hurricanes as a member of the Navy's "Hurricane Hunters" team. *NAVAL AVIATION NEWS*

ARTS AND ENTERTAINMENT

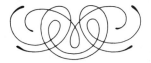

The **1ST ACTRESS** *to win the Academy Award* was Janet Gaynor, who was named Best Actress in 1928. The opulent ceremony to which modern filmgoers and televiewers have grown accustomed wasn't yet a gleam in the eye of the Academy of Motion Picture Arts and Sciences, which staged the affair at a banquet held in a Hollywood restaurant. The acting awards were then based on a complete set of performances for the year instead of on one particular role. For her work in *Sunrise, Seventh Heaven,* and *Street Angel,* Gaynor took home that first gold statuette, later nicknamed Oscar by Bette Davis, one of her successors.

The **1ST** *black* **ACTRESS** *to win an Academy Award* was Hattie McDaniel. A veteran headliner in radio and vaudeville, McDaniel was thirty-six years old when she made her way to Hollywood in 1931. She worked part-time as a maid and washerwoman before landing roles in such films as *Saratoga, Nothing Sacred,* and *Showboat.* But it was her portrayal of Vivien Leigh's mammy in the film version of the Margaret Mitchell novel *Gone with the Wind* that made her famous and brought her the Academy Award for Best Supporting Actress in 1939. After winning the Oscar, McDaniel starred in a long-running television series *Beulah.* She died in 1952.

1ST ACTRESS *to win an Obie* (Village Voice Off-Broadway Award) was Julie Bovasso, who was so honored for her performance in *The Maids*, which opened on May 6, 1955, at the Tempo Playhouse. The actress was also founder and director of the Tempo company, which won an Obie that same year as the best experimental theater of the off-Broadway season. For a short period in 1973, Bovasso directed *In the Boom Boom Room* at the Vivian Beaumont Theater, thus becoming the first female director at the Lincoln Center playhouse.

1ST ARCHITECT was Louise Blanchard Bethune. Born in Waterloo, New York, on July 21, 1856, Louise began designing houses and other structures independently and taught and traveled in preparation for entering Cornell University as an architectural student. Already quite knowledgeable in the subject, she was offered and accepted instead a position as a drafting apprentice with a Buffalo architectural firm. After five years she opened offices of her own with a fellow apprentice, Robert Bethune, whom she later married. Among her designs are an Episcopal chapel, a brick factory, a baseball stadium, many New York schools, and the Lafayette Hotel in Buffalo. She was elected to the American Institute of Architects on April 4, 1888, becoming its first woman member. She died in Buffalo in 1913.

The Lafayette Hotel in Buffalo, New York, shown here at the turn of the century, was designed by America's first woman architect, Louise Blanchard Bethune. It is still in operation today.
LAFAYETTE HOTEL

The **1ST** *syndicated* **CARTOONIST** was Dale Messick, whose comic strip "Brenda Starr" first appeared on June 19, 1940, in the Chicago *Tribune*. It was the first comic strip to feature a woman as the leading character. In the beginning of her career, Messick shortened her name from Dalia to Dale and submitted her cartoons by mail so that newspaper editors couldn't tell that the artist was a woman. The adventures of Brenda Starr, the crusading newspaper reporter, have appeared without interruption since 1940, and are now read by 7½ million people each day. ("Teena," a female comic-strip character created by artist Hilda Terry, appeared in 1941 and ran in Sunday segments for twenty-three years.)

Artist Dale Messick considered making her famous comic-strip character a bandit but changed her mind and created "Brenda Starr, Reporter." Brenda's adventures have appeared in daily newspapers for forty years. CHICAGO TRIBUNE–NEW YORK NEWS SYNDICATE, INC.

© 1969 by The Chicago Tribune World Rights Reserved

The **1ST CLOWN** in the *Ringling Brothers and Barnum & Bailey Circus* was Peggy Williams, a twenty-two-year-old speech pathology major from Madison, Wisconsin, who went to the Ringling Brothers Clown College in 1969 to study nonverbal forms of communication, such as pantomime. She became adept not only at pantomime but at juggling, costuming, makeup, acrobatics, and all the other skills unique to a clown's performance. By graduation time Williams had decided that she could help people more from inside a circus ring than from inside a clinic, so she auditioned and became the first female clown in "The Greatest Show on Earth." In January 1970 she took her first professional pratfalls at the opening show in the company's winter headquarters at Venice, Florida.

1ST CONDUCTOR *on Broadway* was Liza Redfield. A concert pianist from the age of eight, Redfield later spent five years conducting summer productions while trying to convince producers on the Great White Way to give her a break. In 1960, Herb Greene, the co-producer and conductor of the long-running hit *The Music Man,* decided to step down from the podium. He turned the baton over to Redfield, who took over as leader of the twenty-four-piece orchestra at the Majestic Theater on July 4, 1960.

1ST CONDUCTOR *at the Metropolitan Opera* was Sarah Caldwell. Born in Missouri in 1928 and raised in Arkansas, Caldwell began playing chamber music on the violin when she was a toddler and was performing in concerts at the age of six. After completing studies at the New England Conservatory of Music, she decided to become a conductor instead of pursuing the violin. In 1957 she founded the Opera Company of Boston and, as its artistic director, helped launch nearly fifty operas. She raised her baton at the Met for the first time on January 13, 1976, conducting a production of *La Traviata* with Beverly Sills.

1ST LYRICIST *elected to the Songwriters' Hall of Fame* was Dorothy Fields. The daughter of famed vaudevillian Lew Fields, she was strongly advised by her father to stay away from show business. It was, he warned her, too rough. She ignored his advice, however, and became an actress before turning to full-time songwriting in 1920. Among her nearly four hundred songs are such popular hits as "On the Sunny Side of the Street," "Exactly Like You," "Don't Blame Me," and "I Won't Dance." In March 1971 she was one of ten songwriters in the first group elected to the Songwriters' Hall of Fame, and the only woman in the group. Dorothy Fields died in 1974 at the age of seventy.

The 1ST *feminist* **MAGAZINE** *to achieve widespread commercial success* was *Ms.* In 1971, a small editorial group that included feminist Gloria Steinem put together a forty-page magazine that was tucked as a bonus inside the regular issue of *New York*. Women rushed to buy the magazine, which presented articles on how to write a marriage contract and why women fear success, as well as full-page ads inviting them to consider careers as stockbrokers. It sold out immediately. Magazine marketing experts scoffed at the sale, however, saying that it was not a realistic appraisal. They insisted that the average woman across America was not interested in such things and would not buy the magazine. The *Ms.* group thought otherwise, however, and gathered a staff that included Patricia Carbine, then editor-in-chief of *McCall's*, who became the publisher. As the first issues began to go out, subscriptions, advertising, letters of support, and manuscripts began to pour in. Ad revenues rose rapidly, and within a year of its debut

Ms. had stunned its critics by recovering its investment. The magazine expanded its activities within two years to include children's records and a television show, and to introduce a marketing division to help educate advertisers to what women really want. Largely because of the magazine's success, "Ms.," a previously unheard of form of address, gained widespread acceptance for the first time.

The 1ST MISS AMERICA was sixteen-year-old Margaret Gorman from Washington, D.C., who won the title in 1921. The contest had been dreamed up that year by Atlantic City officials as a gimmick to extend the Boardwalk season a week beyond Labor Day. Eight cities sent contestants, and Gorman, a high school sophomore who entered as a lark, was astonished when she won. The bosom fetish,

High school sophomore Margaret Gorman poses on the Boardwalk at Atlantic City in 1921, just after being crowned as the first Miss America.

so important to later competition, was not in evidence that first year. The diminutive winner measured 30–25–32 and weighed only 108 pounds. At 5-foot-1 she remains the shortest person ever to hold the title. There were no scholarships that first year or much else in the way of prizes. The first Miss America went back to finish high school the proud owner of several loving cups, which she either gave away or eventually put to practical use: she recalled later having planted flowers in one; and during the Depression, when she and her husband were struggling to meet household expenses, they melted down another one for the silver.

The **1ST MOVIE DIRECTOR** was Lois Weber, born June 13, 1881, in Allegheny, Pennsylvania. Weber began her career as a pianist, then moved to New York as a teenager to study voice. She landed parts in several stage productions, and while on tour with *Why Girls Leave Home* in 1904 she married the company stage manager, Wendell Smalley. The two acted together in stock and repertory, then returned to New York to work for the motion picture companies, which by then were already experimenting with talking pictures. By 1911 they had branched out from acting and were also writing, directing, and sometimes photographing movies for the New York Motion Picture Corporation, which became a subsidiary of Universal Pictures. In 1917, with her reputation as a director well established, Weber opened her own studio, Lois Weber Productions. Her features

had strong social themes and were sometimes cen-
sored. *What Do Men Want?* (1921) dealt with marital
relationships, *The Angel of Broadway* (1927) was about
prostitution, and *Where Are My Children?* (1916) presented a dramatic case for abortion and birth control.
Lois Weber was highly regarded by her colleagues
and for many years was the only consistently successful woman director in the film industry. She wrote,
produced, and directed hundreds of pictures, the last
of which, *White Heat,* was made in 1934. She died
in Los Angeles on November 13, 1939, at the age of
fifty-eight.

The 1ST NOBEL PRIZE *winner in literature* was
Pearl S. Buck. The daughter of American missionaries, Buck spent most of her life in
China. Through her teaching and writing, she became
an important interpreter of Chinese culture for
those of Western civilizations. She wrote over forty
novels and other works, including *The Good Earth,*
for which she won the Pulitzer Prize in 1932. In 1938
she was awarded the Nobel Prize for literature. She
died in 1973.

The 1ST PLAYWRIGHT *on Broadway* was Zona Gale,
whose play *Miss Lulu Bett* opened at the
Belmont Theater on December 27, 1920, and
ran for 201 performances. The play also won Gale

the Pulitzer Prize for drama for 1920–21, making her the first American woman to be so honored. She died in 1938.

The 1ST black **PLAYWRIGHT** *on Broadway* was Lorraine Hansberry, whose play *A Raisin in the Sun* opened on March 11, 1959, at the Ethel Barrymore Theater. It was her first play and was produced, directed, and acted by blacks at a time when anything with a Negro theme was considered very bad box office. *A Raisin in the Sun* ran for two years, won the Drama Critics Circle Award, was made into a highly successful movie with Sidney Poitier, and returned to Broadway in 1974 as a Tony Award-winning musical entitled *Raisin.* Hansberry's career was destined to be brilliant but brief. After producing two more hits, *To Be Young, Gifted, and Black* and *The Sign in Sidney Brustein's Window,* the gifted playwright succumbed to a sudden, rapid onset of cancer and died in 1965.

The 1ST **PULITZER PRIZE** *winner for fiction* was Edith Wharton, a fashionable young New York socialite who employed themes of social climbing and class distinction in her novels. She began writing in 1904 and shortly thereafter moved to Paris, where she wrote most of her work, including *The Age of Innocence* for which she won the Pulitzer Prize in 1921. In 1935, a dramatization of her story, *Old*

New York, by Zoë Akins won a Pulitzer Prize as *The Old Maid.* She died in 1937. (Broadway playwright Zona Gale was the first female to receive the Pulitzer Prize for drama, also in 1921.)

black **SINGER** *to perform a major role at the Metropolitan Opera in New York was* Marian Anderson. Born in Philadelphia, she sang in her church choir as a child. Her voice was so impressive and her potential so obvious even then that the congregation started a fund to insure her chances for a career. After studying and appearing in concert in America, she went to Europe, where Toscanini proclaimed hers to be the voice of the century. Yet because of racial discrimination, in 1939 she was barred by the DAR from appearing in a concert at Washington's Constitution Hall. Consequently, Eleanor Roosevelt resigned from that organization and sponsored the black woman's appearance at the Lincoln Memorial. Anderson made her debut at the Met in 1955 as Ulrica in *Un Ballo in Maschera.*

TELEVISION *news anchorwoman was* Dorothy Fuldheim, who stepped before the cameras of WEWS–TV in Cleveland, Ohio, in 1947. Fuldheim had been an actress, lecturer, book reviewer, and network radio commentator when Scripps-Howard signed her to anchor the news on WEWS, the first station between Chicago and New

Network radio commentator Dorothy Fuldheim was hired by the Scripps-Howard Broadcasting Company in 1947, as the first television news anchorwoman. WEWS–TV, CLEVELAND, OHIO

York. The sponsor, a beer company, argued that only a man would be appropriate for the job. However, the station stood by Fuldheim, whose style and talent as a newscaster endeared her to Cleveland audiences, and eventually, to the beer company, which sponsored her for the next eighteen years. During her career she interviewed such notables as Adolf Hitler, Jimmy Carter, Jerry Rubin, and Queen Farida of Egypt. By 1979, she was still anchoring Cleveland's six o'clock news and, at age eighty-six had been on the job longer than any other television broadcaster, male or female.

The **1ST** *network* **TELEVISION** *news anchorwoman* was Barbara Walters, who began co-hosting the "ABC Evening News" with Harry Reasoner in September 1976. Born in Boston in 1931, she graduated from Sarah Lawrence and went to work for NBC as a secretary. After seven years she landed an off-camera job as a writer for the "Today" show. After three years she became a regular contributor of on-camera reports and, eventually, a co-host of the show. Her move to ABC brought with it a five-year contract for $1 million a year, making Walters the highest paid TV news personality in history.

The 1ST *theater* **USHERS** seated audiences at the Majestic Theater, located at Broadway and Fifty-ninth Street in New York City. Convinced that the theatrical district would soon expand, William Randolph Hearst built the theater several blocks north of the rest of the district and launched a dazzling premiere production of *The Wizard of Oz* to draw audiences to the new location. He also tried an innovative concept in staffing: women ushers. Costumed in black dresses with bright red sashes over the shoulder, the women seated opening-nighters for the first time on January 21, 1903. Because of its northern location, actors referred to the theater as the Arctic Circle. The location never did become popular, and the Majestic was eventually used as a movie house, then a TV studio. The women ushers caught on, however, and they have remained a part of the Broadway scene ever since.

AVIATION

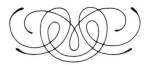

The 1ST AIRPLANE DESIGNER was Lillian Todd of New York City. Todd, who had begun turning out mechanical inventions when still a girl, had a particular interest in flying machines and had even built a working model dirigible. In December 1906 she entered her own full-sized glider-type airship in the Aero Club of America Exhibition. It had pneumatic wheels and a unique system of fans and propellers for controlling flight. Todd's designs attracted serious attention from designers and engineers, but there is no evidence that any of her prototypes ever left the ground. She, herself, never got a chance to learn to fly.

The 1ST AIRPLANE PASSENGER was Mrs. Hart O. Berg who went aloft with Wilbur Wright for a two-minute flight in 1908 at Auvers, France, where her husband had been sent to act as Wright's European representative. Before taking off, Mrs. Berg tied her hat onto her head with a scarf and gathered her full-skirted dress around her ankles with a cord to keep it from blowing around or becoming entangled in the plane's controls. When they landed, the French made little of the flight but marveled at Mrs. Berg's skirt, which remained tied as she walked away from the aircraft. Parisian designers were inspired to create a whole new fashion which they dubbed the "hobble skirt."

Goggles in place, Mrs. L.A. Whitney secures herself into the open cockpit of the guppy-shaped "flying boat" to be whisked across Tampa Bay as America's first female passenger on a regularly scheduled airline. ST. PETERSBURG *TIMES*

The **1ST AIRPLANE PASSENGER** *on a regularly scheduled flight* was Mrs. L. A. Whitney of St. Petersburg, Florida, who made the ten-mile hop over water between that city and Tampa, Florida, on January 8, 1914. The airline had initiated its service only a week before, shuttling one passenger per trip in a Benoist bi-winged "flying boat" across Tampa Bay, which at that time lacked a bridge.

The **1ST AIRPORT MANAGER** was Laurette Schimmoler of Bucyrus, Ohio. In 1932 the tiny town, located in Crawford County, found itself without a soul willing as well as able to run its single-runway airstrip. Schimmoler, a student pilot, was offered the job after every qualified man turned it down. She took charge of the modest air traffic on May 28, 1932, in return for the equally modest salary of ten dollars a week.

The 1ST ASTRONAUT CANDIDATE *tested* was Jerrie Cobb, a twenty-nine-year-old professional pilot from Oklahoma who was recruited in 1959 to secretly undergo tests that were already publicly being taken by John Glenn, Alan Shepard, and other male candidates for the Mercury program. Beginning in 1960, Cobb passed three sets of tests, first at the Lovelace Clinic in Albuquerque, New Mexico, then at a NASA testing center in Oklahoma, and finally at the Naval Aerospace Medical Institute in Pensacola, Florida. Her evaluations were high, sometimes higher than Glenn's, and the doctors rated her suitability for space flight as excellent. But while the agency began to select one man after another, it stalled on giving Cobb an appointment to the space team. When Mary Wallace Funk II and Rhea Allison, the first of twenty-four women pilots scheduled to follow Cobb through the tests, also scored high marks, NASA abruptly canceled all testing on women. Later, it grudgingly admitted to a congressional subcommittee that it had not actually been prepared to have a woman represent the United States in space and had only been testing them experimentally in anticipation of a time when space trips with females would become appropriate.

Jerrie Cobb, the first American woman to undergo astronaut candidate tests, pilots a laboratory training vehicle that simulates the motion of a craft in outer space. NASA

One year later, in 1963, Valentina Tereshkova of the Soviet Union became the first woman to actually make a space flight.

The 1ST **ASTRONAUT CANDIDATES** *selected for training* were announced by the National Aeronautics and Space Administration on January 16, 1978. They were Shannon W. Lucid, 35, a biochemist from Oklahoma City; Dr. Anna L. Fisher, 28, a physician from Rancho Palos Verdes, California; Judith A. Resnick, 28, an electrical engineer from Akron, Ohio, who now lives in Redondo Beach, California; Sally K. Ride, 27, a physics researcher at Stanford University; Dr. Margaret R. Seddon, 30, a Memphis surgeon; and Kathryn D. Sullivan, 26, a geologist from Cupertino, California. All of the women were selected to train as "Mission Specialists," a newly created position for crew members aboard space shuttles. The women would assist in coordinating all operational activities of the craft except the piloting as well as in carrying out on-board research projects.

1ST FLIGHT ATTENDANT was Ellen Church, a nurse and student pilot who convinced Boeing Air Transport, a predecessor company of United Airlines, to take her aboard as a flight attendant. "Don't you think it would be good psychology

Known as the Flying Florence Nightingales, the original airline flight attendants, all registered nurses, pose in uniform along with chief attendant Ellen Church, who dreamed up the idea. Next to Church (upper left) is Alva Johnson. From lower left are Margaret Arnott, Inez Keller, Cornelia Peterman, Harriet Fry, Jessie Carter, and Ella Crawford. UNITED AIRLINES

to have a woman up in the air?" she asked. "How is a man going to say he is afraid to fly when a woman is working on the plane?" Church was hired as chief stewardess and quickly recruited seven other women to work with her. The company required that they be registered nurses, no older than 25, under 115 pounds, no taller than 5-foot-4, and single. The pay was $125 a month for 100 hours of flying time. The stewardesses logged their first flight on May 15, 1930, between San Francisco and Chicago, with four working the first shift as far as Cheyenne, Wyoming, and the other four completing the flight to Chicago.

The **1ST** *black* **FLIGHT ATTENDANT** was Ruth Carol Taylor, a nurse from Ithaca, New York. In 1957, she joined Mohawk Airlines, a regional carrier in the Northeast, which eventually became part of Allegheny Airlines. Her first flight was on February 11, 1958, between Ithaca and New York City.

The **1ST** balloon **PILOT** was Mary H. ("Carlotta") Myers of Mohawk, New York, who made her first ascension on July 4, 1880, near the town of Little Falls. She and her husband, Carl, were among the first Americans to conduct extensive research with lighter-than-air craft and are credited with developing improved balloon fabrics, designing portable hydrogen generators, and experimenting with lightweight cars.

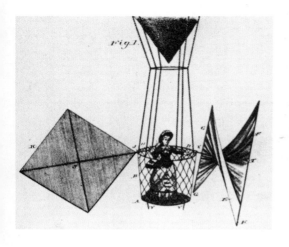

The drawing of the woman in the basket is by Mary H. ("Carlotta") Myers, America's first woman balloonist. It is one of a series that illustrate a method of steering for which she received a patent in the 1800s. NATIONAL AIR AND SPACE MUSEUM, SMITHSONIAN INSTITUTION

In 1886, Mary Myers ascended in a balloon filled with natural gas to an altitude of four miles, an astonishing feat considering that the aircraft was not equipped with oxygen. Her skill at precision landing gained Myers widespread attention, and she remained much in demand as an exhibition balloonist for over thirty years.

The **1ST PILOT** *to fly airmail* was Katherine Stinson. She earned her license on July 24, 1912, the fourth woman in the United States to do so, and began appearing at air shows as a featured performer. On September 23, 1913, Stinson opened an airmail route between the grounds of the Montana State Fair, where she was performing, and downtown Helena. The route, Number 663,002, remained opened with Stinson in charge for a prearranged four days. Stinson was best known for her spectacular flying stunts and was the first woman pilot to loop-the-loop. At a Los

Angeles air show in 1915 she dazzled spectators with a nighttime salute to the state. She spelled out CAL with flares attached to her wings, then lit up the sky over Los Angeles with a series of death-defying loops, spins, and spirals. At the outbreak of World War I, she tried to enlist but was refused because of her sex. Later, she and her younger sister Marjorie (see *First female* **PILOT** *in the U.S. Aviation Reserve Corps* page 51) opened a flying school in San Antonio, Texas. Their mother, Emma, was the business manager. The only flying school to be operated by women, it trained military pilots both for the United States and Canada. Katherine Stinson retired from flying in 1920.

The **1ST PILOT** *to fly regularly scheduled airmail* was twenty-five-year-old Helen Richey. Already a veteran with one thousand hours in the air and a world endurance recordholder, she began her first regularly scheduled flights on December 31, 1934, between Washington, D.C., and Detroit, Michigan. Aboard were seven passengers and a substantial quantity of letters and packages. Disgruntled over her hiring, the men of the Air Line Pilots Association refused to admit her to membership and launched a campaign to have her fired. Defended in the press by Alice Paul and Amelia Earhart, a friend and one-time racing companion, Richey held onto her job for almost a year but was restricted to fair-weather flying. Inactivity and open resentment from the male pilots led to her resignation in 1935. Richey died in New York

City in 1945 at the age of thirty-eight. The Air Line Pilots Association did not admit a woman to membership until 1973 (see *First female* **PILOT** *to fly for a commercial airline,* page 47).

1ST PILOT *to fly for a commercial airline* was Emily Howell Warner of Denver, Colorado, who began regularly scheduled flights as a first officer for Frontier Airlines in January 1973. Warner had been flying professionally since 1960, when she became a flight instructor for Clinton Aviation in Denver. After nine years with Clinton, during which time she became their flight school manager, then chief pilot, she was hired by Frontier. She was elected to membership in the Air Line Pilots Association one year later, becoming its first woman member. Only six months after Warner began flying for Frontier, American Airlines hired Bonnie Tiburzi, a graduate of their flight academy at Ft. Worth, Texas, to fly 727s out of New York. Tiburzi, who had flown professionally for many years, became the first woman to be hired by a major trunk airline, that is, one with an extensive nationwide route system.

1ST PILOT *to fly coast to coast* was Laura Ingalls. She left Roosevelt Field, New York, on October 5, 1930, in her Moth biplane and arrived in Glendale, California, on October 9. She spent

30 hours and 27 minutes in the air and made nine stops along the way. On the return trip, Ingalls shaved nearly five hours off her flight time. Two years later Amelia Earhart would make the trip non-stop (see *First female airline* **PILOT** *to fly solo across the Atlantic*, page 54).

The **1ST PILOT** *killed in a plane crash* was Julia Clark, a native of London, England, who had moved to Denver, Colorado. A graduate of the Curtiss Flying School in San Diego, California, she received her license on May 19, 1912, becoming only the third woman in the nation to do so. Clark promptly joined an exhibition team and flew to Springfield, Illinois, where the group was scheduled to perform at the upcoming State Fair. Just after sundown on June 17, a few days before the first show, Julia took her Curtiss biplane up for a spin. Visibility was poor and her wing hit a tree limb, sending plane and pilot crashing to the ground. Clark survived the fall but died en route to the hospital.

The **1ST PILOT** *to obtain a license* was Harriet Quimby. Born in Coldwater, Michigan, in 1875, she started off as a journalist and drama critic. It was while working as a writer that she became enthusiastic about airplanes and determined

Harriet Quimby, wrapped warmly in one of the hooded flying suits that were her trademark, receives farewell wishes from her crew as she prepares to depart on her solo flight across the English Channel. NATIONAL AIR AND SPACE MUSEUM, SMITHSONIAN INSTITUTION

to learn to fly them. She had become friends with Mathilde Moisant, a pilot whose family operated the Moisant Flying School on Long Island, New York. The school was one of the few in the country that welcomed women students, and she enrolled there. After completing the course, she decided to try for a pilot's license (not a requirement for flying a plane in those days). She passed the licensing test on August 1, 1911, the first woman in the United States and only the second in the world to achieve that distinction. Quimby's greatest acclaim, however, came from flying across the English Channel, which she did on April 16, 1912. She was the first female pilot in the world to cross that particular stretch of water. Enthusiastically received by the French, who were far ahead of everyone else in the field of aviation, Quimby became a celebrity. A flamboyant dresser, she was recognized everywhere in her hooded, plum-colored, satin flying suits. When she returned to the United States, she brought with her a new French monoplane which she had learned to fly in France. On July 1, 1912, shortly after her return, she participated in the Boston-Harvard Aviation Meet. She was taking a short flight over Dorchester Bay around Boston Light with the manager of the event as her passenger when suddenly, without warning, the plane flipped over out of control. Both Quimby and her passenger were thrown to their deaths. Ironically, the empty plane righted itself and landed uneventfully and undamaged.

The 1ST PILOT *to fly at night* was Ruth Law who earned her license on November 12, 1912. A year later she took a moonlight flight over Staten Island, New York, and was so impressed with the theatrical possibilities that she decided to specialize in nighttime exhibitions. Her air shows were so spectacular that before long she was famous, earning nine thousand dollars a week for her death-defying stunts. In December 1916, floodlights were thrown onto the Statue of Liberty for the first time and Law performed for President and Mrs. Wilson, whose yacht was anchored nearby for the occasion. With the word "Liberty" emblazoned on the underbelly of her plane, she dazzled the presidential party with overhead spins and dives that brought her within two hundred feet of their boat, throwing a shower of sparks across the harbor. When Law tried to enlist during World

By special permission and at the request of the U.S. government, aviator Ruth Law wore her Army uniform when appearing on recruitment tours. NATIONAL AIR AND SPACE MUSEUM, SMITHSONIAN INSTITUTION

War I, she was rejected because of her sex but was asked by the Army and Navy to fly officially as a recruiter, which she did. When traveling in that capacity, she wore the uniform of a noncommissioned Army officer, the first woman in U.S. history to do so. While on a goodwill tour of Japan, China, and the Philippines in April 1919, Ruth Law flew the first airmail into Manila.

The **1ST PILOT** *in the U.S. Aviation Reserve Corps* was Marjorie Stinson. At the time of her induction she was only nineteen years old and the youngest licensed pilot in the country. The sister of famed aviator Katherine Stinson (see *First female* **PILOT** *to fly airmail*, page 45), Marjorie had gone to Orville Wright for instruction, but because of her age, he would not let her fly until her mother wired permission. Two months later, Marjorie soloed, and a week after that she earned her license. In 1915, the same year that she served in the Air Reserve, Marjorie opened an aviation school in San Antonio, Texas, with her sister and mother. Besides U.S. military pilots, their pupils included the cadets of the Royal Canadian Flying Corps who became known as the Texas Escadrille because of their training with Stinson. When the school closed in 1918, Marjorie went to Washington, D.C., where she became an aeronautical draftsman for the Navy.

The 1ST PILOT *to fly solo* was Blanche Stuart Scott. Nineteen-year-old Scott gained public attention in 1910 by making the first solo transcontinental auto trip by a female driver. During the New York–San Francisco trip, she witnessed an airplane-flying demonstration that fired her interest in the new machines. Immediately upon her return to New York she proceeded upstate to the Keuka Lake Field in Hammondsport for training. The instructor, Glenn Curtiss, reluctantly agreed to allow her behind the controls, but only to "cut the grass," that is, to taxi around the field without taking off. He even placed a mechanical device on the engine's throttle to prevent it from attaining enough speed for flight. After repeating this humiliating exercise for a number of days, Scott became impatient. On September 2, 1910, the device on the throttle of her plane "somehow" became

Blanche Stuart Scott learned to operate a plane in 1910, but her instructor didn't think that she, or any woman, should actually be allowed to fly. She took off anyway, becoming the first woman to solo, later gaining fame as a daring stunt flyer. AIR FORCE MUSEUM; NATIONAL AIR AND SPACE MUSEUM, SMITHSONIAN INSTITUTION

disengaged, and when she taxied down the field the plane lifted off the ground and rose to an altitude of forty feet. With her disgruntled and apprehensive teacher watching from below, she made a brief, uneventful flight and brought the plane smoothly back to earth. Six weeks later Blanche Scott made her professional debut as a stunt pilot, billed as "The Tomboy of the Air." She thrilled crowds at air shows by flying her plane upside-down only twenty feet off the ground, dipping underneath bridge spans, forming figure eights, and making her famous "death dive," plummeting straight down toward the earth from an altitude of four thousand feet and pulling back on the stick only when she was within two hundred feet of crashing. Until 1916, Scott continued to do exhibition flying and testing but her increased frustration over the lack of opportunities for women in aviation led her to retirement at the age of twenty-seven, when she became a news commentator. She died in 1970 at seventy-nine, angry to the very last at the public attitudes and conditioning that discriminated against female flyers.

The **1ST PILOT** *to fly solo across the Atlantic* was Amelia Earhart, born July 24, 1898, in Atchison, Kansas. Earhart had crossed the Atlantic in 1928 as a passenger but was not satisfied with that mild entertainment. Earhart had become a licensed pilot eight years earlier, while working as a photographer to pay for lessons and to buy a secondhand plane. After the Atlantic crossing, Earhart became determined to earn the accolades that had come her way merely because she had been on board the plane. She perfected her skills over the next few years and made plans to fly the ocean on her own. On the afternoon of Friday, May 20, 1932, she donned jodhpurs, a silk shirt, and a leather flying suit, tucked a can of tomato juice and a thermos of soup into the cockpit, and took off from Harbour Grace, Newfoundland, before the

Amelia Earhart, the first woman to make solo flights across both the Atlantic and Pacific oceans, poses in front of the Lockheed Electra in which she was later lost at sea. THE NEW YORK PUBLIC LIBRARY PICTURE COLLECTION

sun set. Though her instruments failed and she was forced at one point to fly perilously close to the water in order to see, she touched down in the pasture of a startled Irish farmer 14 hours and 56 minutes later, announcing unceremoniously, "I've come from America." She was bundled into an automobile and bustled six more miles to the nearest telephone, where the news of her arrival was announced.

In August of that same year Earhart made the first nonstop transcontinental airplane flight. Only a year before, A.E., as she was called, had made the first transcontinental flight in an autogyro, the predecessor of the helicopter, which at that time was still in the developmental stage. She left Newark, New Jersey, on May 29, 1931, arrived in Oakland, California, on June 6, and returned to Newark on June 22. She had spent 150 hours in the air and covered 11,000 miles in the primitive chopper.

Earhart was also the first woman pilot to fly the Pacific Ocean. Amid a flurry of controversy over the advisability of allowing her to make such a dangerous flight, she left Wheeler Field in Honolulu, Hawaii, on January 11, 1935. Averaging 133 miles per hour over the 2,408-mile stretch of water, she made a smooth landing 18 hours and 16 minutes later in Oakland, California. While attempting to fly around the world in 1937, her plane vanished, and Amelia Earhart was presumed lost at sea. She was thirty-nine years old.

The **1ST PILOT** *to fly solo around the world* was Jerrie Mock, a thirty-eight-year-old Columbus, Ohio, aviator. Piloting a single-engine red and white plane dubbed the *Spirit of Columbus*, she took off from the Columbus airport on March 19, 1964. Making twenty-one stops, she circled the globe and touched down again in Columbus on April 17. She had flown 22,858.8 miles in twenty-nine days. A veteran pilot of many years, Mock had been the first woman to fly solo across the Pacific in a single-engine plane. (Amelia Earhart made the first solo trip in a twin-engine Vega.) For her circumnavigation of the earth, Mock received the Federal Aviation Agency's Decoration for Exceptional Service. It was presented to her at the White House on May 4, 1964.

Jacqueline Cochran, the first woman to break the sound barrier, stands beside the Lockheed F–104G Super Starfighter in which she had just flown at more than twice the speed of sound. Cochran holds more world aviation records than any human being in history.

1ST PILOT *to break the sound barrier* was Jacqueline Cochran. A native of the Florida panhandle, Cochran rose from a childhood of extreme poverty and hardship to become one of the most accomplished pilots the world has ever known. Founder and leader of the only all-female squadron of ferry and transport pilots to fly for the United States during World War II, she later piloted military jets and helped in the planning of the space program. Cochran broke the sound barrier on May 18, 1953, when she flew a North American Canadair F–86 over Roger's Dry Lake, California, at a speed of 652.337 miles per hour. Eleven years later, at the age of fifty-seven, she piloted a Lockheed F–104G Super Starfighter through the same California desert skies at a record-shattering 1,429.2 miles per hour, more than twice the speed of sound. She was the first woman to win the Bendix International Air Race, and to date she holds more world aviation records than any other pilot, male or female.

The **1ST PILOT'S ORGANIZATION** was the Ninety-Nines, which met for the first time on November 2, 1929, in a hangar at Valley Stream, Long Island. Among those who gathered were Louise Thaden, the first woman finisher of the Bendix Air Race, and Amelia Earhart. Earhart became the group's first president, and it was she who suggested that their name depend on the number of women pilots who responded to their invitation to join. For a while it looked as though they would become the Eighty-Sixes, but thirteen last-minute applications made it the Ninety-Nine Club. During World War II the WASPs, headed by Jacqueline Cochran (see *First female* **PILOT** *to break the sound barrier*, page 57, and *First female military* **PILOTS** *to fly for the United States*, page 18), relied heavily on the ranks of the Ninety-Nines for personnel.

BUSINESS
AND FINANCE

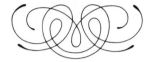

The 1ST BANK *in the United States* opened in Clarksville, Tennessee, on October 6, 1919. Its president, Brenda Vineyard Runyon, who dreamed up the idea, and all the remaining staff members, including the janitor, were women. They had no trouble selling stock and began operations with capital stock of $15,000. The bank was highly successful for seven years, at which time Runyon became ill and could no longer continue as president. With no remaining director able or willing to assume her role, the women decided to liquidate. They gave back their depositors' money, paid investors the profits, and on June 8, 1926, merged with the First Trust and Savings Bank of Clarksville, which is still in existence.

The 1ST BANK *of New York* opened at Fifty-seventh Street and Park Avenue in Manhattan on October 16, 1975. Committed to providing a full range of banking services to both women and men on a nondiscriminatory basis, the new bank also offered such unusual services as a library of consumer, financial, and women's publications, and a conference room for use by women's and other groups. On opening day over a thousand people swarmed into the bank, mostly women who had been denied credit in their own names or in some other way been unfairly treated at other banks. The president, Madeleine McWhinney, had come to her job after a number of other career firsts: she had risen through the ranks of the Federal Reserve System to become its first woman officer and had been the first woman president of the New York University School of Business Administration.

The **1ST BANKER** was Maggie Lena Walker, born in 1867 in Richmond, Virginia. The daughter of a former kitchen slave, young Maggie helped support her family by delivering the laundry that her mother took in for a living and by caring for her younger brother. An outstanding pupil, she completed high school in 1883 at the head of her class and began teaching elementary school while taking business courses at night. In 1899 she became executive secretary-treasurer of the Independent Order of St. Luke, a black insurance cooperative. Under her leadership the organization bought an office in Richmond, added twenty-four state chapters to its membership, and boasted $3 million in paid claims. In 1903 the Order established the St. Luke Penny Savings Bank with Maggie Walker as president. Highly successful, it absorbed other black Richmond banks, to become the Consolidated Bank and Trust Company in 1929. For reasons of health, Walker stepped down as president at that time but continued to head the board of directors until her death in 1934. Today a Richmond street, high school, and theater are all named in her honor.

In July 1979 the U.S. Treasury began circulating the new Susan B. Anthony one-dollar coin. Some merchants complained that it looked too much like a quarter and refused to accept it. U.S. MINT

The 1ST *pictured on a U.S.* **COIN** was suffragist Susan B. Anthony. The one-dollar coin was released on July 2, 1979. Treasury officials had first considered picturing only a representative female figure such as Miss Liberty, but American feminists lobbied for the honoring of a real individual. After much deliberation, Anthony was selected over Nellie Tayloe Ross (see *First woman* **GOVERNOR,** page 88), Jane Addams (see *First female* **NOBEL PEACE PRIZE** *recipient*, page 75), and Eleanor Roosevelt.

The 1ST *pictured on American* **CURRENCY** was Lucy Holcombe Pickens of La Grange, Tennessee. Miss Holcombe was married at the age of twenty-five to Francis Wilkinson Pickens, a South Carolina political leader twenty-seven years her senior. At the outbreak of the Civil War he became governor of his state, and in that same year, at the suggestion of the Southern Treasury Secretary, C. G. Memminger, Lucy Pickens's picture was engraved on the Confederate one-hundred-dollar bill. For thirty years after her husband's death in 1869, she single-handedly managed their estate near Edgefield, South Carolina. In 1899 she died and was buried there, with former slaves as her pallbearers.

Lucy Holcombe Pickens became the first American woman to have her image engraved on currency when she was chosen by Confederate Treasurer C.G. Memminger for the Confederate $100 bill, which was first issued in 1861. (The engraving was based on a marble bust of her, which had been sculpted in Russia.) FAYETTE COUNTY HISTORICAL SOCIETY

The 1st pictured on U.S. **CURRENCY** was Martha Washington, whose picture was engraved on the one-dollar bill of 1886. She was also the first American woman to have her image appear on a U.S. postage stamp. The lilac-colored eight-cent stamp was issued on December 6, 1902.

The 1ST *black* **MILLIONAIRE** was Sarah Breedlove Walker, born in 1867 to sharecropping parents in the Louisiana delta. Widowed and a mother before the age of twenty, she was supporting herself and her daughter by taking in laundry for $1.50 a day when she decided to create a line of hair products especially for black women. Working at home, she formulated shampoos, oils, conditioners, and a host of other items designed to be used in combination with each other and applied according to her hot-comb method. The venture soon grew too successful for home production and she moved to Denver, started door-to-door sales, and trained a team of assistant "beauty culturists" to help her. By 1908 she had married Charles Walker, a newspaperman, and began using the name Madame C.J. Walker. She set up a factory in Denver and opened a second office in Pittsburgh,

Madame C. J. Walker, shown at the wheel of her automobile, started out doing laundry for $1.50 a day but wound up a millionaire before the age of fifty by marketing her own line of hair preparations. *EBONY* MAGAZINE

which her daughter managed. Her company now employed three thousand people, many of them women who wore smartly styled uniforms and sold door-to-door as Walker agents. By 1914, Madame C.J. Walker was a millionaire with a town house in Harlem and a country estate at Irvington-on-Hudson just north of the city. But she did not forget her own beginnings and contributed substantially to many charities, including the NAACP, the YWCA, and several homes for the aged. She also maintained scholarships at Tuskegee Institute in Alabama to help give young black women the education she had been denied. She became ill while on a business trip in 1919 and died on May 25, shortly after returning to her home at Irvington-on-Hudson.

The **1ST PATENT HOLDER** was Mary Kies of South Killingly, Connecticut. In 1808 she came upon what she thought to be a unique method for successfully weaving straw and silk or thread together and sent her idea to the U.S. Patent Office in Washington, D.C., for verification. On May 5, 1809, she was granted a patent.

The **1ST PROSTITUTES UNION** was COYOTE (acronym for Call Off Your Old Tired Ethics), founded in San Francisco, California in 1972 by Margo St. James, a former prostitute. St. James, who gave up the profession to become a private detective, started the union to help protect prostitutes against rape, assault, murder, and other abuses, and to work for legalization of the profession. It was, she said, a woman's issue since the abuse of prostitutes grew out of men's fear of not being able to control women. Within five years, membership in the organization had grown to twelve thousand worldwide, and when they held their annual Hookers Convention in San Francisco, panel discussions were well-attended, not only by members but by sociologists, lawyers, religious and civic leaders, anthropologists, and law-enforcement officials.

The **1ST PUBLISHER** *of the Declaration of Independence* was Mary Katherine Goddard, who was also America's first woman postmaster. Goddard grew up in the publishing business. Her mother, Sarah Updike Goddard, was publisher of the Providence *Gazette* and her brother ran the *Maryland Journal and Baltimore Advertiser,* where Mary worked as a journalist. When he left in 1774 to take a job with the Colonial postal service, Mary took over as editor and publisher. During the Revolution many newspapers were forced out of business, but Mary—who was not only a fine editor, but also an expert typographer—managed to keep her paper alive. She did this partly by accepting outside jobs, two of which would make her famous. In 1775 she became postmaster of the Annapolis-Baltimore postal station becoming the first American woman to hold that job.

She continued to run the paper at the same time. In 1776 when the members of Congress decided that the Declaration of Independence should be made known to citizens in every state, they asked Mary Goddard to print copies of the document. She continued in the dual roles of postmaster and publisher until 1784, at which time she turned the newspaper back to her brother. She remained in the postal service until 1789 when the new federal government was formed. (The first woman postmaster to be hired after the adoption of the Constitution was Sarah deCrow, who managed the Hertford, North Carolina, station beginning in 1792.)

The 1ST **STOCK EXCHANGE DIRECTOR** was Mary Gindhart Roebling, president of the Trenton Trust Company of New Jersey since 1937. She became a director of the American Stock Exchange on October 28, 1958. She was one of thirty-two governors of the exchange and one of only three public members not already connected with the Wall Street community.

The 1ST **WORLD'S FAIR** was held in Chicago, Illinois, the week of April 18–25, 1925. Earlier, in 1893, another Chicago fair, the World Columbian Exhibition, had included women. At that time one exhibition hall was designed by a woman, Sophia Hayden, to house all the activities then deemed appropriate for women, such as crafts and needlepoint. In 1924, several Chicago women decided that women's participation in industry demanded better representation. They raised money and traveled to other cities, enlisting the help of many women in the project. Seventy different industries were represented at the 1925 fair in exhibits designed and run by the women themselves. President Calvin Coolidge sent Vice-president and Mrs. Dawes to the fair. Asked for his comments, he expressed dismay that the women had launched the project themselves without asking the government to subsidize it.

EDUCATION

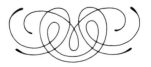

The 1ST COLLEGE was Mount Holyoke Seminary, South Hadley, Massachusetts, which opened in 1837 with eighty students and two teachers. The first graduation was the following August, celebrating a class of four members. They were Martha Abbott, Sarah Brigham, Abigail Moore, and Persis Woods. The school's first director was Mary Lyon, who was the principal and not the president. Hence, by the time the institution's name had been changed to Mount Holyoke College in 1893, Frances Willard of the Evanston College for Ladies in Illinois had become known as the nation's first female college president.

The 1ST COLLEGE PRESIDENT was Frances E. Willard, born near Rochester, New York, in 1839. From an early age Frances had a healthy dislike for the behavior expected of her as a female. In a gesture of contempt that disgraced her family, she cut off her hair and announced that she wanted to be called Frank, a nickname she kept through life. Her father, a stern disciplinarian, reluctantly agreed to her education, and in 1859 she graduated from the North Western Female College in Evanston, Illinois. After teaching and traveling in Europe for some time, she returned to her alma mater to become a professor there. In 1871 the school became the Evanston College

Frances E. Willard, America's first female college president and a Woman's Christian Temperance Union leader, rides a two-wheeler to promote the virtues of abstinence and clean living. NATIONAL WOMAN'S CHRISTIAN TEMPERANCE UNION

for Ladies, and Willard was named its president. All the members of the faculty and all the trustees were women, a fact that could not have been more pleasing to Willard, who had become deeply devoted to educating women. However, it caused some concern at nearby Northwestern University, which managed to take over and absorb the women's college in 1873. Willard was made dean of women, but thereafter her authority was constantly challenged, and she finally decided to resign a year later. She became an advocate of temperance, president of the Illinois Woman's Christian Temperance Union, and in 1891, president of the

World WCTU, an organization that soon boasted a membership of 2 million women. Willard saw the union as a means of interesting women in politics and was highly effective in forming alliances with various suffrage factions. Shortly after a trip to England, Willard became ill and died in a New York City hotel. She was only fifty-eight. Two thousand mourners packed her funeral in that city, and twenty thousand filed past her casket at a second service at the Woman's Temple in Chicago. Her motto, left to the WCTU and at one time their slogan was "Do Everything."

The **1ST NOBEL PEACE PRIZE** *recipient* was Jane Addams. Born on September 6, 1860, she attended the Rockford Female Seminary in Rockford, Illinois, graduating at the head of her class in 1881. Originally intending to go into medicine, she spent only a year at the Women's Medical College of Pennsylvania, partly because of failing health. After a serious spinal operation, she was disabled for six months and then began traveling to recover her health. On a trip to Europe with her close friend and former Rockford roommate Ellen Gates Starr, she became aware of the plight of the poor in many countries and witnessed the devastating social consequences of rapid industrialization. In London she visited Toynbee Hall, a model settlement house founded by students from Oxford. She returned to the United States determined to live and work among the poor, disenfranchised, and needy. With Starr's help she searched

Chicago's West Side until she located a dilapidated mansion that had once been owned by a wealthy businessman, Charles Hull. She bought it, moved in, and opened its doors to the neighboring immigrant population. Hull House became a center for social reform, and Jane Addams gained worldwide respect for her efforts. On December 10, 1931, she was awarded the Nobel Peace Prize (she shared the award with Dr. Nicholas Butler, president of Columbia). An ardent feminist, Addams donated the money to the Women's International League for Peace and Freedom, which she had helped found. She died four years later, on May 31, 1935. She left her estate to the first-born girl baby of each succeeding generation.

The **1ST RHODES SCHOLARS** *from the United States* began their studies at Oxford University in October 1977. Under the provisions of the will of British financier Cecil Rhodes, who died in 1902, the scholarships had for seventy-two years been awarded only to men. It took an Act of Parliament in 1975 to make women eligible recipients. Among the seventy-two scholars in 1977 were thirteen American women. They were: Maura J. Abeln, Vassar College; Caroline E. Alexander, Florida State University; Catherine Lynn Burke, the University of Virginia; Nancy Lee Coiner, Yale University and Providence College; Diane L. Coutu, Yale University; Sarah Jane Deutsch, Yale University; Laura Garwin, Harvard University; Sue M. Halpern, Yale University and Smith College; Daryl

Koehn, the University of Chicago; Alison Muscatine, Harvard University; Mary Cargill Norton, Michigan State University; Suzanne Perles, Princeton and Harvard universities; and Denise Thal, Harvard University. In addition to the American women, there were four female Rhodes scholars from Canada, three from Australia, and one each from New Zealand, South Africa, India, and West Germany.

1ST SORORITY was Alpha Delta Pi. The group, considered to be a secret society, was formed by sixteen women at Wesleyan College in Macon, Georgia, on May 15, 1851. They named themselves the Adelphian Society and adopted the motto "We live for one another." In 1904 the Adelphians voted to change their name to Alpha Delta Phi, which was changed again in 1913 to Alpha Delta Pi.

POLITICS, LAW, AND LAW ENFORCEMENT

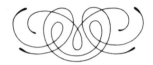

1ST CABINET *member* was Frances Perkins, who was born in Boston in 1880 and appointed Secretary of Labor by President Franklin D. Roosevelt in 1933. After receiving her master's degree from Columbia University in 1910, Perkins worked for the New York Consumers League and became interested in labor and social reform. Her interest was heightened after she witnessed the famous Triangle Shirtwaist Factory fire in 1911, in which 146 people, mostly women, died. Appointed by then Governor Roosevelt to the New York State Industrial Commission, she lobbied tirelessly for the improvement of factory working conditions. In 1913 she married Paul Wilson but chose to retain her own name. When her U.S. Cabinet appointment came in 1933, union leaders strongly objected, not only because she was a woman, but because she had not come from within their own ranks. She fought, however, for employment compensation, child labor laws, minimum wages, and old age pensions and was instrumental in the passage of the Social Security Act of 1935 and the Fair Labor Standards Act of 1938. After leaving the Cabinet in 1945, she lectured at Cornell University. She died in 1965.

1ST *Secretary of Commerce in a U.S.* **CABINET** was Juanita Kreps, a Duke University professor and labor economist appointed by President Carter in December 1976. Kreps was born in a small coal-mining town in eastern Kentucky. Her family was poor, and she worked her way through Berea College, a small self-help school that specialized in aiding disadvantaged students. Partly because of her own poverty and because she was attracted to the orderliness and precision of the subject, Kreps became interested in economics; after graduating in 1942, she went to Duke and earned a master's degree and a Ph.D. in the field. She taught in California, Ohio, and New York before returning to Duke as a professor and dean of the women's college. Although she was a specialist in labor economics, Dr. Kreps was also an acknowledged expert in income distribution, manpower, and problems of the aging. She wrote ten books, including *Sex in the Marketplace: American Women at Work* and *Women in the Economy: A Look at the 1980s*. She was also the first woman director of the New York Stock Exchange.

The **1ST** *Secretary of Health, Education and Welfare in a U.S.* **CABINET** was Oveta Culp Hobby, a Texas lawyer and newspaperwoman. Hobby went to work for the War Department in Washington, D.C., in 1941 and was asked to help make plans for a women's army corps. When President Roosevelt created the Women's Army Auxiliary Corps (WAACS), he made Hobby its leader. Holding the rank of Colonel, she retained leadership of the corps when it changed from auxiliary status to the regular Women's Army Corps (WACS) in 1943. She retired from that position in 1945. In 1953 when President Eisenhower created the Department of Health, Education and Welfare, he appointed Oveta Culp Hobby its first secretary.

The 1ST Secretary of Housing and Urban Development in a U.S. **CABINET** was Carla Anderson Hills. Born in Los Angeles in 1934, she worked her way through Yale Law School, then went back to California, where she opened a practice and became one of the state's most prominent trial attorneys. In 1974, she became Assistant Attorney General in the Justice Department's Civil Division in Washington, D.C., and on March 10, 1975, President Gerald Ford appointed her Secretary of HUD to replace James Lynn, a Nixon appointee. She remained in the Cabinet post until President Ford left office, at which time she was succeeded by Patricia Roberts Harris, the first black woman in the Cabinet.

The 1ST **CONGRESSWOMAN** was Jeannette Rankin, elected to the U.S. House of Representatives by the Republicans of Montana in 1916. Rankin served there until March 4, 1919, when she was defeated for re-election, partly because of her outspoken anti-war sentiments. She continued to work for women's rights, however, and in 1940 was again returned to Congress, where she remained until 1943.

She was the only member of Congress to vote twice against the United States's entry into war. The first time was on April 6, 1917, against World War I, and the second was on December 8, 1941, against World War II. She never gave up her fight for peace, and in 1968 she led an anti-war protest on the Capitol steps in Washington, D.C. She died on May 18, 1973, at the age of ninety-three.

The **1ST** *black* **CONGRESSWOMAN** was Shirley Chisholm, elected to the U.S. House of Representatives from New York in 1968. She was born Shirley St. Hill on November 30, 1924, in the Bedford-Stuyvesant section of Brooklyn. Her parents were West Indian immigrants who worked as laborers to put their children through school. Shirley earned a scholarship to Brooklyn College and went on to Columbia for a master's degree in education. Intending to make a career in that field, she began as a nursery school teacher. That led her to a job as director of a day-care center, which in turn led her to a strong involvement with women and the feminist movement, the sources of her greatest support when she decided to enter politics. "Stick to teaching," she was told by males and those she described as Uncle Tom females, "and leave politics to the men." But New York feminists were excited by her feisty outspokenness. They helped elect her to the New York State legislature in 1964 and the U.S. House of Representatives in 1968. After taking office on January 3, 1969, Congresswoman Chisholm drew national attention to the needs of domestic workers for the first time, pushing through a bill that guaranteed minimum wages to this group (mostly black women). She annoyed party regulars by announcing in 1972 that she intended to run for president, and then seriously pursuing the nomination. At the convention she drew 154 delegate votes. Chisholm then ran and was re-elected to her congressional seat for a second, and later a third term.

The **1ST** *avowed lesbian* **COUNCIL MEMBER** *elected to a city council* was Kathy Kozachenko, a senior at the University of Michigan at Ann Arbor. In April 1974 she ran and was elected to the city council of that city from a ward predominantly populated by students. Chairwoman of the County Advisory Committee on Women, Kozachenko did not regard her sexuality as a campaign issue. "I hope to reach all women," she told the press, "especially those who normally take little interest in politics."

The **1ST** **COUNCIL PRESIDENT** *in New York City* was Carol Bellamy, also the youngest person and the first woman elected to a citywide post there. Bellamy, who grew up in Plainfield, New Jersey, graduated from Gettysburg College in Pennsylvania. She spent two years as a Peace Corps volunteer, then returned to New York City where she studied and became a lawyer. In 1971 Bellamy ran for the New York State Senate and was elected for three successive terms. New York feminists became early Bellamy supporters, but few others paid any attention to her, even when she announced plans to seek the council seat. Ignored by the press, Bellamy revived a style of street campaigning she had used in earlier senatorial races. Week after week she stood outside shopping centers and department stores, stopping passersby with a smile and a handshake, and stationed herself at subway stops in the wee hours of the morning to greet commuters stepping off their trains. Her efforts paid off when she toppled longtime incumbent Paul O'Dwyer in the primary and went on to win the election. Once in office, Bellamy turned a job that had formerly had little significance into one of importance, establishing herself as an ombudsman between City Hall and the public. Before she had served a year in office, party leaders were predicting a future of practically unlimited possibility for Carol Bellamy. She could, they decided, have just about any office she wanted. She could become mayor of New York, governor of the state, or perhaps go even higher than that.

Emma Edwards Green studied painting in New York City but returned to her native state of Idaho, where she was commissioned to design the state seal.

The 1ST DESIGNER *of a state seal* was Emma Edwards Green. She studied art in New York City in the late 1800s, then moved back to her native Idaho to paint. In July 1890, Idaho joined the Union and Emma Green was commissioned to design a picture to be used as the state seal. She completed it that year, and it was approved in 1891.

The 1ST DISTRICT ATTORNEY was Annette A. Adams. Born in 1877, she was one of California's first women school principals. In 1910 she became a student again, earning a law degree. She then went into private practice, and in 1918 she became the first woman D.A. (for the Northern California district). In 1920 President Woodrow Wilson appointed her an assistant to the U.S. Attorney General. When she died at seventy-nine, Adams was presiding judge of the Third District Court of Appeals and California's ranking woman jurist.

The 1ST GOVERNOR *whose husband did not precede her in office* was Ella T. Grasso. Born in Windsor Locks, Connecticut on May 10, 1919, she was the only child of Italian immigrant parents. Ella seemed suited at an early age for political life, according to her classmates, who in one high school yearbook predicted that she would become mayor of the town. She went instead to Mount Holyoke College, graduated Phi Beta Kappa in economics, got married, and joined the League of Women Voters. Before her first child was two years old, Grasso was elected to the Connecticut Assembly. She was then thirty-three years old. In 1959 she became the Connecticut Secretary of State, and in 1970 she went on to the U.S. Congress for two successive terms. Grasso had once told reporters that she didn't think a woman could manage a family and the governorship at the same time, but her own experiences in office and the fact that her children were almost grown changed her mind. She ran for governor in 1974, defeating her male opponent by a wide majority. She took office on January 8, 1975, and served for four years, after which she sought and won re-election to a second term.

The **1ST GOVERNOR** was Nellie Tayloe Ross, who succeeded her late husband as governor of Wyoming in 1924. She was defeated for re-election in 1926. Nellie Ross was also the first director of the U.S. Mint.

The **1ST** *white* **INDIAN CHIEF** was Harriet Maxwell Converse, an author, folklorist, and passionate defender of Indian rights. She was born near Elmira, New York, in 1836. In 1881, Converse and her husband became close friends of General Ely

S. Parker, a Seneca sachem (chief) who was then Commissioner of Indian Affairs. The Converses visited the Cattaraugus reservation of the Seneca Nation, where they met Parker's Wolf Clan. Harriet Converse became totally committed to preserving the Indian culture, and in 1891 she directly intervened with the passage of a bill by the New York legislature that would have broken up reservations in the state. In 1902 she led a massive letter-writing campaign to the U.S. Congress that saved the Senecas from being charged a $200,000 land liquidation fee. She had been adopted by the clan in 1885, but in 1891 the Indians formally changed her name to Ya-ie-wa-noh, meaning "She Who Watches over Us," and made her a Seneca sachem. As an honorary chief of the Six Nations, she was admitted to the secret Little Water Medicine Society. When she died in 1903, representatives from the Six Nations gathered at the Episcopal church in New York where her funeral was held and performed the Iroquois ritual burial rites. Her collections of Indian relics at the American Museum of Natural History and the Museum of the American Indian in New York, as well as at the Peabody Museum at Harvard University, are considered major contributions to the preservation of Indian lore in America.

The **1ST JUDGE** *in the U.S. Court of Appeals for the Second Circuit* was Amalya L. Kearse, who was sworn in on June 27, 1979, in New York City by Chief Judge Irving R. Kaufman. At forty-two she was also one of the youngest persons to sit on the Second Circuit, which is often considered the most important court in the country after the Supreme Court.

The **1ST** *black federal* **JUDGE** was Constance Baker Motley. Born in New Haven, Connecticut, in 1921, she was the ninth in a family of twelve children. As a civil rights lawyer in the early 1960s, she worked tirelessly to eliminate state-enforced segregation in the South and successfully argued nine civil rights cases before the U.S. Supreme Court. Later she became the first black woman elected to the New York State Senate, and the first to serve as Manhattan borough president. In 1966, at the recommendation of Senator Robert F. Kennedy, President Lyndon Johnson appointed her judge of the U.S. District Court for the Southern Division of New York. After some delay caused by a Southern senator who objected to her appointment, she was confirmed on August 30 of that year.

The **1ST** **JUSTICE OF THE PEACE** was Esther McQuigg Morris, born in 1814 near Spencer, New York. In 1869 she and her second husband, John Morris, settled in South Pass City, Wyoming, where he went into business and she became an outspoken advocate of women's rights. That year, at a time when the national suffrage movement was still in its infancy, she convinced leaders of the Wyoming legislature that suffrage would encourage more women to move into the territory. They not only gave the women of Wyoming the vote, but passed other laws allowing married women to control their own property and giving female teachers the same pay as their male colleagues. On February 14, 1870, Esther Morris was appointed Justice of the Peace of South Pass City. She held the job for almost nine months. Apparently personal problems led to her early retirement. She separated from her husband after charging him with assault and battery and left town the next year. In 1873 she was nominated for the Wyoming legislature but decided not to run. She did remain an active reformer well into her eighties, however, and after a meeting with Susan B. Anthony in 1895 became a delegate to the national suffrage convention. She died in Cheyenne in 1902 at the age of eighty-seven.

The 1ST National **LABOR UNION** was the Daughters of Saint Crispin, an organization of shoemakers. The membership of eight hundred women in the trade convened in Lynn, Massachusetts, on July 28, 1869, and elected Carrie Wilson of Lynn their president. In March 1870 they joined in a public demonstration with male shoemakers, marching through the streets of the town in a snowstorm to protest poor wages. By that time their ranks had grown to nearly a thousand women.

The Daughters of Saint Crispin, a shoemakers' union, march for fair wages in Lynn, Massachusetts, in 1870.
LIBRARY OF CONGRESS

1ST LAWYER was Arabella Babb Mansfield. After graduating from Iowa Wesleyan University in 1866, she apprenticed in a law office for three years, then took the Iowa bar exam. She passed with high scores but was not automatically admitted to the bar, as were her husband, John Mansfield, and other men who took the test. The Iowa Code stated that admission was open to any qualified "white male." This was taken to mean that no one else was eligible. A judge disagreed, however, and in June 1869 she was admitted to the bar. The next year the words "white male" were removed from the statute. Ironically, Belle Mansfield never practiced law. Instead, she went back to school for a master's degree, studied law in London and Paris, and returned to Iowa to become a law professor. She died in 1911.

The **1ST** *black* **LAWYER** was Charlotte E. Ray, who graduated from the Howard University School of Law in 1872 and was admitted to the bar in Washington, D.C., on April 23 of that year.

The **1ST** **LAWYER** *to present a case before the U.S. Supreme Court* was Belva Lockwood, a pacifist and equal rights activist, born near Niagara Falls, New York, in 1830. In her forties Lockwood sought admission to two different law schools but was refused by both because of her sex. A third, the National University Law School in Washington, D.C., allowed her to complete the course but would not grant her a degree until requested to do so by the President of the United States, Ulysses S. Grant, to whom Lockwood had appealed. Admitted to the bar, she attempted to plead her first case before the Supreme Court in 1873 but was refused on grounds of custom. Lockwood lobbied Congress, gained the support of women's rights advocates, and secured the passage of a bill that would ensure the right of a woman to pursue cases all the way through to the highest courts in the land; having done so, she returned once again to the U.S. Supreme Court and on May 3, 1879, resumed her case. In 1884 a California women's convention nominated Lockwood for President of the United States. She drew over four thousand votes, even without the support of Susan B. Anthony and other suffragists who disagreed with her opinion that the Nineteenth Amendment was unnecessary. In her last appearance before the Supreme Court at the age of seventy-six, she argued a claim for the Eastern Cherokee Indians, which brought them an award of $5 million. Belva Lockwood died in Washington in 1917 at the age of eighty-six.

Lawyer Belva Lockwood was the first woman to practice before the U.S. Supreme Court. LIBRARY OF CONGRESS

1ST *black* **LAWYER** *to present a case before the U.S. Supreme Court* was Violette N. Anderson of Chicago, who was admitted to practice on January 29, 1926.

1ST *avowed lesbian* **LEGISLATOR** was Elaine Noble, a twenty-eight-year-old Harvard graduate who was elected to the Massachusetts General Assembly from Boston in 1974. Noble made her homosexuality known at the outset of her campaign but did not make a particular issue of it since she was not running as a gay candidate. Her greatest support came from members of her own Boston community and in particular from elderly citizens for whom she worked especially hard during her four years in office. Her seat was abolished in 1978 as a result of redistricting.

1ST **MAYOR** was Susanna Medora Salter, who was elected mayor of Argonia, Kansas, on April 4, 1887. Her name was placed on the ballot in jest by a group of local merchants who were angry over her attempts to close down the beer halls. The citizenry, particularly her sisters in the Woman's Christian Temperance Movement, responded by giving her a two-thirds majority of the vote. She served a one-year term and was paid a token fee of one dollar.

1ST POLICE DETECTIVE was Isabella Goodwin, a former matron of the New York City Police Department. After sixteen years in that position, she was finally promoted to Acting Detective Sergeant First Grade on March 1, 1912. She then served for twelve more years as one of New York's Finest without a single promotion, retiring on October 31, 1924.

1ST PRESIDENTIAL CANDIDATE was Victoria Claflin Woodhull, born in Homer, Ohio, on September 23, 1838. Quick-witted and adventurous, she claimed to be clairvoyant and traveled for several years with her younger sister, Tennessee, as a spiritualist and healer. In 1868 they opened a highly successful brokerage firm in New York City, the first women in the nation to do so. The enterprising sisters then turned to publishing with the radical magazine *Woodhull and Claflin's Weekly*, which regularly discussed such taboo subjects as abortion, prostitution, and venereal disease. In 1872, Victoria founded the Radical Reformers Party, which nominated her for President of the United States on May 10 of that year. The nomination took place in New York City's Apollo Hall. Though highly publicized, as were all her ventures, Woodhull's political career was not successful. She was shunned by all factions, in the end by feminists as well, because of her outspoken advocacy of free love. At one point, she was openly living with both her former and current husbands under the same roof. In 1901 she moved with her sister to Tewkesbury, England, where she died on June 9, 1927, at the age of eighty-eight.

Victoria Claflin Woodhull and her sister, Tennessee, published a radical magazine and ran the first woman-owned brokerage on Wall Street. Woodhull later founded the Radical Reformers Party, which in 1872 made her the first female U.S. nominee for President. SOPHIA SMITH COLLECTION, SMITH COLLEGE

1ST **PRISONER EXECUTED** *for crimes against the government* was Mary Surratt. She was convicted without a trial and hanged as a conspirator in the assassination of President Abraham Lincoln. Surratt, a widow, ran a boardinghouse in Washington, D.C. where her son, a Southern sympathizer, and his friend John Wilkes Booth sometimes met. In the hysterical aftermath of Lincoln's death, she was rounded up along with three other alleged conspirators and questioned before a nine-member military tribunal. Although she could not be directly implicated, she was nevertheless found guilty and sentenced to die because, according to President Andrew Johnson, she "kept the nest that hatched the egg." Two young volunteer lawyers tried unsuccessfully to have her sentence commuted, but she went to the gallows on July 7, 1865, still proclaiming her innocence.

The 1st **PRISONER EXECUTED** *in the electric chair* was Martha M. Place, who had been tried and convicted of murdering her stepdaughter, Ida, in Brooklyn, New York, on February 7, 1898. After being imprisoned at Sing Sing in Ossining, New York, for a year, she was electrocuted on March 20, 1899.

The 1st **QUEEN** *of American descent* was Queen Geraldine of Albania. Born August 6, 1915, in Hungary, she was the daughter of Virginia Gladys Stewart, an American, and Julius Apponyi, a Hungarian count. Geraldine, a countess, became the bride of King Zog of Albania on April 28, 1938, at the Albanian Royal Palace in Tirana.

1ST SENATOR was Rebecca Latimer Felton from Decatur, Georgia, an eighty-seven-year-old advocate of women's rights. She was also the first woman from that state to become a member of Congress. Born in 1835, she was appointed to the Senate on October 3, 1922, by Governor Thomas Hardwick, who had opposed women's suffrage and was hoping by the gesture to gain the support of women voters. She attended two sessions of the Senate, on November 21 and 22, 1922, before a successor was elected. She died on January 24, 1930, at the age of ninety-five.

1ST *elected* **SENATOR** was Hattie Ophelia Wyatt Caraway. A native of Bakerville, Tennessee, she married a college classmate, Thaddeus Caraway, who was elected to the Senate from Arkansas in 1920. When Thaddeus died in 1931, the governor of Arkansas appointed Hattie to serve out the remainder of her husband's term with the understanding that she would vacate the office upon its expiration. But after assuming her duties and functioning for some time with considerable success and popularity, Senator Caraway surprised her colleagues by announcing her decision to seek re-election. She won a decisive victory in the heaviest primary vote ever recorded in Arkansas and was returned to office for another six years. She was also the first woman to preside over the Senate, doing so briefly on May 9,

1932, and again on October 19, 1943, when she opened the proceedings and presided as president pro tempore in the absence of Vice-president Henry Wallace. Also the first woman to chair a committee and the first to conduct a Senate hearing, she left office on January 3, 1945, having been defeated by J. William Fulbright. Senator Caraway was the third woman from Arkansas to serve in the U.S. Congress. She died on December 21, 1950.

1ST SENATOR *to succeed a woman Senator* was Hazel Hempel Abel, a Republican from Nebraska, who replaced Senator Eve Bowring, also a Republican, on November 8, 1954. Abel had been elected six days earlier to fill the two-month balance of Senator Bowring's term.

1ST *to be granted the* **VOTE** lived in Wyoming. As a territory in 1869 it had decided in its first legislative session to extend the vote to women. The move was largely the result of persuasive arguments presented to legislators by Esther Morris of South Pass City, who convinced them that it would be good business, would encourage law and order, and would attract new settlers to the area. She later became the country's first female justice of the peace (see *First female* **JUSTICE OF THE PEACE,** page 90). Following adoption of the legislation, which also

granted property rights to married women and pro-
vided for equal pay for female schoolteachers, the
women of Wyoming cast their first ballots in the 1870
elections.

The **1ST VOTER** in America was Mrs. Josiah Taft of
Uxbridge, Massachusetts. Mrs. Taft was a
widow and not entitled to vote. But that right
did fall to her male descendants, and because her only
son, Bazaleel, was underage, she was allowed to cast
a ballot in his behalf in a 1756 election to approve
taxes.

The **1ST WOMEN'S RIGHTS CONVENTION**, called by
Elizabeth Cady Stanton and Lucretia Mott,
took place in Seneca Falls, New York. Hundreds of women gathered there on July 19–20, 1848,
to hear Stanton and others outline, for the first time
in public, a declaration of the inequities suffered by
women under the law. Today, a women's museum and
archives have been established at Seneca Falls, considered the birthplace of the women's rights movement
in America.

RELIGION

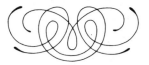

The 1ST MINISTER *ordained into a recognized denomination* was Antoinette Brown, born in 1825 in Henrietta, New York. She pursued the study of theology, an unheard-of discipline for a woman, at Oberlin College in Ohio. The institution, considered radical in its day for accepting both women and blacks, admitted her to the course but would not grant her a diploma upon completion, nor issue her a student license to preach. These double standards awakened her to feminism. She and fellow student Lucy Stone openly challenged the school's policy of requiring women to study debate while at the same time prohibiting them from actually debating. (They won the right to debate each other, an event that drew such crowds it had to be called off.) For three years afterward, Antoinette preached and lectured widely. On September 15, 1853, she was ordained a minister of the First Congregational Church in Butler, New York. She voluntarily left after a year, however, since her own growing feminism and religious liberalism conflicted with the more conventional requirements of being a pastor. Two years later she married Samuel Blackwell, brother of the feminist physician, Elizabeth, but refused to give up either her preaching or women's rights activities. She died in 1921 at the age of ninety-six.

The 1ST American-born **NUN** was Mary Terpin, a young woman of Canadian and Indian descent who was born in Illinois in 1731. When she was seventeen, her parents sent her to live and study with the Ursaline sisters at New Orleans (see *First* **NUNS,** below) and within a year she had decided to become one of them. In the summer of 1749 she entered the convent as a postulant and five months later received her habit. On January 29, 1752, she took her vows and assumed the religious name of Sister St. Martha. Several years later she contracted tuberculosis and never recovered. She died in 1761, only thirty years of age.

The 1ST **NUNS** *to establish a permanent convent in the United States* were the Ursalines, a French order originally formed in Italy during the sixteenth century. In 1639 the first Ursaline missionaries went to Quebec, Canada. Later, a settlement of Jesuits in New Orleans asked the French order to send a second delegation to start a school for girls in that city. In 1727 a dozen sisters, led by Mother Superior Marie Tranchepain, arrived. The nuns established a convent and school in a small two-story wooden structure located in what is today known as the French Quarter. Rebuilt in 1750, the convent and gardens still stand today but no longer shelter the sisters, who now occupy larger quarters some blocks north of the original convent. There the nuns continue to operate the Ursaline Academy, a school for young women.

The **1ST** *Episcopal* **PRIESTS** were ordained at the Episcopal Church of the Advocate in Philadelphia on July 29, 1974. At that time the eleven women, who were already Episcopal deacons, received holy orders. A year later a second group was ordained in Washington, D.C., bringing the total to fifteen. Though accepted by their respective dioceses, the women were not officially recognized by the Church until 1976 when a general convention in Minneapolis voted to clarify the canon as including women as well as men. The next year the Reverend Jacqueline Means, a chaplain at the Indianapolis Women's Prison became the first woman to be ordained with the official sanction of the Church.

The **1ST** **RABBI** was Sally Preisand. She graduated from the Jewish Institute of Religion of the Hebrew Union College at Cincinnati, Ohio, in June 1972, and was ordained there that same month. She then accepted an appointment to the Stephen Wise

Free Synagogue in New York City, where she became assistant rabbi. An activist, Rabbi Preisand championed women's rights and joined other religious leaders in denouncing nuclear proliferation. For her outstanding contributions, especially her work with Jewish youth, Rabbi Preisand received many Woman of the Year awards. In 1973 the Temple Israel in Columbus, Ohio, also deemed her *Man* of the Year.

The **1ST** *American-born* **SAINT** was Elizabeth Bayley Seton, born August 28, 1774, into a staunchly Episcopal New York City family. At the age of twenty, she married a wealthy young merchant, William Seton. They had five children. On a trip to Europe in 1803, William died, leaving Elizabeth a widow at twenty-nine. She stayed on in Italy for several months with some Catholic family friends. They encouraged her to convert to their faith, which she did within a few years of her return to America. The move brought strong opposition from her friends and relatives, many of whom abandoned her altogether. Severed from financial support for herself and her children, she took them and moved to Baltimore, Maryland, where she was welcomed and invited to start a school for girls. The following year, 1809, at Emmitsburg, Maryland, she became a nun. As Mother Seton, she then founded the first American order of the Sisters of Charity. Seton and her sisters trained teachers, opened orphanages, and founded the nation's first free parochial school, where her own children became boarders. She died at Emmitsburg on January 24, 1821. She was beatified in 1963 by Pope John XXIII, and canonized in 1975 by his successor, Paul VI.

At 30, Elizabeth Bayley Seton was a widow with five children when she converted to Catholicism, became a nun, and founded the American Sisters of Charity. THE AMERICAN SISTERS OF CHARITY

The **1ST** *naturalized American to become a* **SAINT** was Mother Frances Xavier Cabrini, who came to the United States from Italy in 1889. She founded the Missionary Sisters of Charity, built a network of hospitals, and for many years devoted herself to helping the nation's immigrant poor. She became a citizen in 1909 and died of malaria eight years later in New York City. On July 7, 1946, she became a saint, the first U.S. citizen to be canonized.

SCIENCE
AND MEDICINE

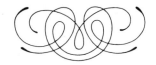

1ST *member of the* **AMERICAN MEDICAL ASSO- CIATION** *(AMA)* was Sarah Hackett Steven- son, who was born in Buffalo Grove, Illinois, in 1841. A student of Mary Harris Thompson (see *First female* **SURGEON,** page 122), she graduated from the Women's Hospital Medical College of Chicago in 1874. Two years later, while practicing in Chicago, she was chosen by the Illinois State Medical Society as a del- egate to the AMA convention in Philadelphia. Admitted to the convention, she became its first woman member. She was also the first woman appointed to the staff of the Cook County Hospital in Chicago, and the first woman appointed to the Illinois State Board of Health. Dr. Stevenson died in Chicago in 1909.

1ST **ASTRONOMER** was Maria Mitchell. Born in the New England sailing town of Nantucket, where knowledge of the stars was critical to daily life and livelihood, Mitchell, while working as a schoolteacher and librarian also became expert in the study of astronomy. For many years she and her father, who was well known in the field, worked in their observatory. In October 1847, she sighted a new comet, which was later named for her. As a result of her work and that discovery, she was elected to the American Academy of Arts and Sciences, its first woman member. The founders of Vassar College per-

Maria Mitchell, shown here in her observatory at Vassar College, was America's first woman astronomer. VASSAR COLLEGE

suaded her to join their first faculty by tempting her with an observatory of her very own, complete with the most advanced equipment. She accepted the position and became popular as an educator, influencing many young women to pursue the subject of astronomy. Maria Mitchell died in 1889.

The 1ST *Pilgrim aboard the* Mayflower *to give* **BIRTH** *in the New World* was Susanna White. Shortly after sighting Cape Cod, the voyagers dropped anchor at what is now Provincetown Harbor in order to explore the site for possible settlement. While there, on November 20, 1620, White gave birth to a son, whom she called Peregrine. Earlier at sea, another woman, Elizabeth Hopkins, had delivered a son named Oceanus.

The 1ST *proponent of* **BIRTH CONTROL** in America was Margaret Sanger, a nurse. While working among the poor in New York City, she became aware of the financial pressures upon the lower classes created by large families. In 1914 she began setting forth her ideas in a monthly newsletter, *The Woman Rebel,* and calling for birth control. The newsletter was banned as obscene literature, and Sanger had to leave the country to escape imprisonment. When the charges were dropped in 1916, she returned to the United States and continued her crusade, opening the first birth-control clinic in the nation with her sister, Ethyl Byrne. Located on New York's Lower East Side, the clinic was shut down by the police because "obscene materials" (contraceptives) were being dispensed there. This time Sanger spent a month in jail. But gradually her cause was taken up by the medical community, and by 1930 fifty-five similar clinics had been opened across the country. A founder of the International Planned Parenthood Federation, Sanger died in 1966 at the age of eighty-three.

The **1ST DENTIST** was Dr. Emeline Roberts Jones, who in 1855 began to learn dentistry from her husband, a practicing dentist in Danielsonville, Connecticut. After training with him for four years while also acting as his assistant, she became his partner, specializing in the treatment of women and children. After her husband's death in 1864, Dr. Emeline Jones ran the practice on her own. At that time a degree in dentistry was not a requirement for practicing the profession.

The **1ST DENTIST** *to earn a dental degree* was Dr. Lucy Beaman Hobbs, born in 1833 in Franklin County, New York. In 1859, Lucy Hobbs gave up a teaching career to study medicine but was refused admittance to medical school because she was a woman. A sympathetic professor at the college agreed to tutor her privately in some subjects but advised her to consider dentistry, which he believed to be a more suitable occupation for a woman. The idea appealed to her and she began to study at once, apprenticing at the same time with a Chicago dentist. After mastering all the basic techniques and procedures, including the administration of anesthesia, she then applied to the Ohio College of Dental Surgery in 1861, but once again she was refused admittance because of her sex. She then moved to Iowa, opened a practice, and gained wide respect from fellow dentists and from the Iowa State Dental Society, which elected her to membership in 1865. That year she reapplied to the dental college which had refused her and was accepted into the senior class. While there she served as an assistant and advisor to other students because of her knowledge and expertise and was granted her degree after only four months of study. After practicing briefly in Chicago, she married and moved to Lawrence, Kansas, where she taught her husband enough dentistry so that he could join her in a practice. She died in Lawrence at the age of seventy-seven.

The **1ST** *automotive* **ENGINEER** was Marie Luhring, who received her master's degree from Cooper Union in New York City on June 5, 1922. Already an amateur engineer and designer of cars, Luhring had distinguished herself as an undergraduate two years earlier by becoming the first woman elected to the American Society of Automotive Engineers. After earning her master's degree, Luhring started work at the bottom of the profession, as a draftsman for the International Motor Company.

The **1ST** *locomotive* **ENGINEER** was Evelyn L. Newell. A native of West Germany, Newell had become fascinated by trains as a child, and after a brief career as a stewardess with TWA she traded her wings for a job as a station agent in a Wisconsin train yard. A few years later she moved to California just as Southern Pacific was opening up jobs at the head of the train to women. Newell started as a fireman, then went to the company's school for engineers to learn how to drive a locomotive. After many months of work with simulators, and practice in local freight yards, Newell graduated to the main lines. In January 1974 she began driving the 5,000-ton, 128-car Southern Pacific freight trains up and down the winding California coast.

The **1ST** **MEDICAL SCHOOL** was the Boston Female Medical School, which opened its doors to twelve pupils on November 1, 1848. It was founded by a man, Samuel Gregory, who also started the first women's medical society later that month. Called the Female Medical Educational Society, its purpose was "to provide and promote the education of midwives, nurses and female physicians and to diffuse among women generally a knowledge of physiology and the principles and means of preserving and restoring health." The school later became the New England Female Medical College, (See also *First black woman* **PHYSICIAN,** page 121), which in 1874 became part of the Boston University School of Medicine. Meanwhile, 250 miles away at the Medical Institute of Geneva, New York, Elizabeth Blackwell was on her way to becoming America's first female physician (see *First female* **PHYSICIAN** *to earn a medical degree,* page 120).

The **1ST** *American* **NOBEL PRIZE** *winner in science* was Gerty T. Cori, a physician and biochemist who moved to the United States from Czechoslovakia in the 1920s. A research associate and professor at the Washington University School of Medicine, she collaborated with her husband for twenty years in the study of carbohydrate metabolism and enzymes. For their contributions in this area, the Coris were awarded the Nobel Prize for physiology and medicine in 1947. Dr. Cori died ten years later at the age of fifty-one.

The **1ST** **PHARMACIST** was Dr. Susan Hayhurst, who received her degree from the Philadelphia College of Pharmacy in 1883. Already a practicing physician, Dr. Hayhurst had been one of the early graduates (class of 1857) of the Women's Medical College of Pennsylvania. That school is the only one founded for women that is still in operation today as an independent institution, although it now admits male students and is called simply the Medical College of Pennsylvania.

1ST PHYSICIAN *to earn a medical degree* was Elizabeth Blackwell. Though she was refused admittance to twenty-nine medical schools and publicly ridiculed for her attempts, Blackwell persisted. She studied privately for three years before being admitted to the Medical Institute of Geneva, New York, after the director had passed her application on to the students for approval. Thinking it to be a joke, they agreed on October 20, 1847, that ". . . the application of Elizabeth Blackwell to become a member of our class meets our entire approval." Her arrival at the school was greeted with shock and hostility, however. She was cursed, spat upon, refused lodging at first, and barred from some classroom demonstrations. Yet she graduated at the head of her class on January 23, 1849, continued her studies in London and Paris, and returned to New York City, where she opened a dispensary in 1853. Called the New York Infirmary for Women and Children, it was staffed entirely by women. With the help of her younger sister, Emily, by then also a doctor, she added a medical college for women in 1868. Later she returned to England, where in 1875 she helped found the London School of Medicine for Women. She died in Hastings, England, on May 31, 1910, at the age of eighty-nine.

The **1ST** *black* **PHYSICIAN** was Susan Steward, who received her M.D. degree in 1870 as the valedictorian of her class at the New York Medical College for Women. Within the year, Dr. Steward opened a family practice in Brooklyn; her patients included both blacks and whites. She later took advanced studies at the Long Island College Hospital, where she was the only woman in her class. Dr. Steward practiced medicine for forty years, during which time she married twice and raised her children. She died in 1918 at the age of seventy-one. Rebecca Lee is sometimes referred to as the first black woman physician. She attended the New England Female Medical College in Boston in 1863 and 1864, and was granted a "Doctress of Medicine" degree, yet she completed only a ten-week course of study. Most medical courses at the time, even for those who had studied privately, were of a year's duration or longer, so it is likely that Rebecca Lee was actually graduated as a nurse or midwife.

The **1ST** *White House* **PHYSICIAN** was Dr. Janet G. Travell. She was appointed to the post by President John F. Kennedy shortly after he took office in 1961. Dr. Travell, who lectured on pharmacology and orthopedics at Cornell, had been Kennedy's personal physician before he became President, and he credited her with having cured him of a serious back ailment. She was the first civilian White House physician since Warren G. Harding's administration.

The 1ST **SURGEON** was Dr. Mary Harris Thompson, who was born near Fort Ann, New York, on April 15, 1829. As a young woman, she paid for her own education by teaching certain courses to others. Having studied anatomy and physiology on her own, she went to the New England Female Medical College in Boston to increase her knowledge enough to add those subjects to her teaching repertoire. She became so interested in medicine, however, that she decided to make a career of it. After finishing the two courses, she went to New York and interned for a year with the Blackwells (see *First female* **PHYSICIAN** *to earn a medical degree,* page 120). She returned to Boston to complete her medical degree in 1863, and began her practice in Chicago that same year. By 1865 she had founded the Chicago Hospital for Women and Children, establishing herself as head of the medical and surgical staff. Dr. Thompson specialized in abdominal and pelvic surgery, and she developed an abdominal needle that became widely used by other doctors. However, in spite of her proven ability, she was turned down when she sought advanced training at Rush Medical College in Chicago. As a result, she later helped found a women's medical college that became part of Northwestern University. It was not until 1882, when she had been practicing for twenty years, that she gained sufficient acceptance to be elected vice-president of the Chicago Medical Society. For a time one medical journal continued to refer to her as "Miss Doctoress Thompson." Dr. Thompson died in Chicago in 1895 of a cerebral hemorrhage. She was sixty-six years old.

1ST TELEGRAPH OPERATOR was Sarah G. Bagley. An early labor union organizer, she was hired to manage the New York and Boston Magnetic Telegraph Association office in Lowell, Massachusetts, when service was initiated between that town and Boston on February 21, 1846. Unfortunately, however, no one recorded her first message. She was also active in distributing literature to prospective users of the new communication system, which had been introduced commercially only two years earlier by Samuel Morse. At one point, she helped give public demonstrations in which sample messages were hammered out from an auditorium stage. Bagley, positioned in the balcony, would receive, translate, and call them out for the audience to hear.

1ST TELEPHONE OPERATOR was Emma Nutt. She was hired on September 1, 1878, by The Telephone Despatch Company of Boston, a burglar-alarm supplier that also serviced about sixty telephone subscribers. The job had originally been performed by teenage boys whose rough ways and rude manners had alienated a number of the company's customers. As a result, the manager offered the job to his neighbor, Emma Nutt, for a salary of three dollars a day. Customers responded at once to her mannerly "Hello," and her sister Stella was added to the staff that same day, becoming the second female operator. In time, the company became the New En-

Emma Nutt, the first female telephone operator, began connecting parties over the wire on September 1, 1878. AMERICAN TELEPHONE AND TELEGRAPH

gland Telephone and Telegraph Company. Stella left the job after a few years, but Emma stayed at the switchboard and eventually became a chief operator. She finally hung up her headset in July 1911 after thirty-three years of service in "the operating room," as it was called. She died in Cambridge, Massachusetts, in 1926 at the age of seventy-seven.

The 1ST **VETERINARIAN** was Dr. Elinor McGrath, who graduated from the Chicago Veterinary College in 1910. An assistant veterinarian for the state of Illinois, Dr. McGrath practiced in Chicago for thirty-seven years. In 1947 she moved to Hot Springs, Arkansas, where she turned her attentions to the treatment of alligators and ostriches. She also served for many years as the president of the Women's Veterinary Medical Association. She died in Hot Springs on June 19, 1963, at the age of eighty-five.

SPORTS
AND RECREATION

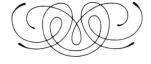

The 1ST ATHLETE *to earn $100,000 in a year* was Billie Jean King. After fifteen years of playing tennis for little or no prize money, in 1972 she broke the $100,000 mark. It was not only a victory for King, a leader in the financial fight of women tennis pros (who often drew the largest crowds but received the smallest prizes), but an economic turning point for all of women's tennis. Because of her leadership, other players began demanding more equitable earnings, and within five years a number of them, including King, had overall earnings in the millions. Also in 1972, she was named Sportswoman of the Year by *Sports Illustrated* magazine, the first

The first American woman to win a singles championship at Wimbledon was Helen Wills Moody. After claiming that title seven times, she won it for the eighth and last time (below) in 1938. WIDE WORLD

woman ever chosen for the honor. In 1979, King added another first by winning her twentieth Wimbledon title (six singles, ten doubles, and four mixed doubles). Until that year she was tied for the record of nineteen wins with Elizabeth "Bunny" Ryan, the first American woman to win at Wimbledon, in 1914. The first American woman to win a Wimbledon singles title was Helen Wills Moody, who in 1927 won the first in a string of eight championships, and the first black American woman was Althea Gibson, who won in 1957 and 1958.

The 1ST AUTO DRIVER *in the Indianapolis 500* was Janet Guthrie. A physicist, Guthrie had been racing for thirteen years before she got her first chance to drive in the Indy, considered the world's toughest auto race. In May 1976 she passed her rookie test at Indianapolis but was unable to race when her car developed mechanical problems during a qualifying round. Guthrie was disappointed but not discouraged. She left immediately for the NASCAR Grand National 600 at the Charlotte, North Carolina, speedway, climbed into a car she had not set eyes on until that day, and without using a relief driver, finished the 600-mile endurance race fifteenth in a field of forty top male drivers. It was the first time a woman had competed against men in a major American stock car race. The next year Guthrie went back to Indianapolis with a new car. She not only qualified, but stunned her disapproving male competitors by finishing ninth against thirty-three of the world's most famous drivers.

1ST BASEBALL *player on a high school varsity team* was eighteen-year-old Linda Williams, of Houston, Texas. A talented rightfielder, Williams had been practicing with the Wheatley High School Wildcats during preseason training in 1978 when the University Interscholastic League forced her to stop because of her sex. On March 25, three days before the opening game of the season, however, a Houston judge ordered the league and the Houston Independent School System to reinstate her. After the game, coach Eugene Jones said of Williams, "She's one of my best three or four outfielders and one of my better hitters." (On March 7 of that same year, Robin Petrini stepped in to pitch two innings for the Capuchino High School team of San Bruno, California, but she was not a regular member of the team.)

1ST *Little League* **BASEBALL** *players* filed the first lawsuit challenging the constitutionality of the league's "no girls" rule on June 28, 1973, in Detroit, Michigan. On that date, lawyers went to court for Carolyn King, a twelve-year-old centerfielder who had beat out fifteen boys for a starting position with the Ypsilanti Orioles but was told that the team's charter would be revoked if she tried to play. The Detroit courts dismissed the case, claiming that they had no jurisdiction, but not before newspapers from coast-to-coast ran the story. Within weeks the national Little League headquarters in Williamsport, Pennsylvania, was bombarded with similar lawsuits from other young players. Late in June of the following year, after most teams had already been selected for the season, the Little League announced a policy change allowing girls to play but leaving the decision of whether to comply up to the local teams. Some did, but most continued to find ways of keeping girls out of their dugouts. Finally, on September 7, 1974, the national organization signed an order agreeing to ban sex discrimination in its local chapters. By that time, some of those young women from Michigan had outgrown the age limit for playing, but because of their efforts thousands of others turned out for Little League tryouts the following spring.

The **1ST BASEBALL** *pitcher on an organized male team* was Virne Beatrice "Jackie" Mitchell. Born in Chattanooga, Tennessee, in 1904, Mitchell was pitching curves at the age of six. By the time she was seventeen, she had gained such a reputation for her pitching that she was signed by the Chattanooga Lookouts, who were hoping to cash in on the inevitable publicity that would follow. Mitchell took her job seriously, however, and when she was called to the mound for the first time during an exhibition game with the New York Yankees, she struck out both Lou Gehrig and Babe Ruth. Though openly scornful of her presence, Ruth struck twice at a ball Jackie described as "dropping just before it gets to the plate." Then she fooled him with a straight one down the middle. "He didn't say anything," she recalled. "He just threw down the bat and walked away."

1ST BASEBALL *team on record* was the Dolly Vardens of Philadelphia, Pennsylvania. Organized in 1867, they shocked fans by appearing on the diamond in red calico dresses that terminated well above the ankle. No gloves were needed since the Vardens played with a ball made of yarn.

1ST *professional* **BASEBALL** *leagues* were formed in the early 1940s when wartime vacancies in the major-league teams created a demand for more players to keep the ball parks in business. In 1943, chewing gum heir Philip Wrigley organized the All American Girls Baseball League, four teams of outstanding women softball players who were paid fifty to eighty-five dollars a week to play. Wrigley did not approve of the unladylike behavior he saw in some of his best recruits, however, and on the first day of training at Chicago's Wrigley Field, he gave them makeup, posture, and etiquette lessons instead of batting practice. He not only banned short haircuts and tomboyish dress but also promised to oust any player who drank or smoked in public. Despite the restrictions, many outstanding women remained with the league. The women played with a ball measuring 11 inches in circumference, smaller than a softball but larger than a regulation baseball, which measured 9. The caliber of play was high, and the women's games were well attended by crowds that routinely numbered up to four thousand fans. A Chicago Cubs manager once remarked after watching six-

In 1941, "Boots" Klupping Ortman, an elementary-school teacher from Maywood, Illinois, pitched one night a week for Parichy's Bloomer Girls, a semi-pro baseball team.

teen-year-old shortstop Dottie Shroeder of the South Bend Blue Sox play, "If that girl were a man, she'd be worth fifty thousand dollars to me." Other leagues soon formed with teams like Parichy's Bloomer Girls, the Rockola Music Maids, and Bidwell's Bluebirds, though their games were more like regular softball than baseball. When the war ended, however, homecoming vets returned to claim the playing fields, and the women players went back to amateur softball. By 1958 the professional baseball leagues for women had disappeared altogether.

1ST BASKETBALL *game played at Madison Square Garden* took place on Saturday, February 22, 1974, between two of the top women's college teams in the country: Queens College of New York and Immaculata College, a Catholic women's school near Philadelphia. Garden officials didn't think that a women's game would draw many spectators so they scheduled it as an opener to a men's game. Nearly twelve thousand fans turned out, and any doubts about who they had come to see were erased when the women's game ended and most of the crowd left. Immaculata's Mighty Macs, under the guidance of coach Kathy Rush, edged out Lucille Kyvallos's Queens team for a 65–61 victory. Women's college basketball was first introduced at Smith in 1892.

1ST *professional* **BASKETBALL** *league,* the Women's Basketball Association, was formed in 1977 and held its first player draft in July 1978 in New York City. There were four teams in the Eastern Division: the Dayton Rockettes, the New York Stars, the New Jersey Gems, and the Houston Angels (Houston was included in the East to help even out the divisions). Teams in the Western Division were the Milwaukee Does, the Chicago Hustle, the Iowa Cornettes, and the Minnesota Fillies. Among the top players selected were Karen Logan of the Red Heads, a professional exhibition team, and volleyball star Mary Jo Peppler. Among the top college draftees were Debbie Mason and Althea Gwyn of Queens College in New York. The first WBA game was played on

December 9, 1978, in the Milwaukee Arena. A crowd of nearly eight thousand watched Chicago win over Minnesota, 92–87.

The 1ST Olympic **BASKETBALL** *team from the United States* competed in the 1976 summer games in Montreal, Canada. It was the first time that this event had been open to women. The fourteen-member U.S. team included the top amateur players, who were chosen by nationwide eliminations. The group had only weeks to train together before going to Hamilton, Ontario, in June for a series of qualifying rounds from which they emerged triumphant and optimistic. And one month later in Montreal, they won an Olympic silver medal for the United States. The team was guided all the way by coach Billie Jean Moore of Fullerton, California. The first Olympic basket scored by an American woman was made by Lucia Harris from Delta State College in Mississippi. The other team members included: Cindy Brogdon, Nancy Dunkle, Vera Haigh, Patricia Head, Charlotte Lewis, Nancy Lieberman, Gail Marquis, Anne Meyers, and Mary O'Connor.

The 1ST six day **BICYCLE RACE** was held in Madison Square Garden in 1896. The event drew a chilly response from sports reporters, who scolded the young contestants, saying they were "old enough to know better" and reminded the public that the League of American Wheelmen, which stood for "all that was best in cycle racing," did not countenance contests between females. Nevertheless, some three hundred curious spectators showed up to watch the women pedal away from the starting line at five minutes past midnight on January 6, 1896. The competitors rode nine-hour shifts with six-hour breaks in between. Interest in the race grew, and by the time the clock struck midnight on January 12, ending the contest, four thousand onlookers were in the stands. All thirteen of the original starters finished the race, and the winner, Frankie Nelson, wheeled over 418 miles.

The **1ST CAMP FIRE GIRLS** were organized by Charlotte V. Gulick. In 1908 she bought a large piece of land on Lake Sebago near South Casco, Maine, and turned it into a camp for girls, thematically based on Indian lore and ceremonies. She named the camp WoHeLo, taking the first two letters of the words *Work, Health,* and *Love.* In 1910 she began working with her husband, Luther Gulick, and William Langdon, both of whom had recently helped organize the Boy Scouts, to form a similar group for girls. She called it the Camp Fire Girls and adopted the name of their camp, WoHeLo, as the watchword. The organization was formally announced on March 17, 1912, just one week after Juliette Low held the first meeting of the Girl Guides (see *First* **GIRL SCOUTS,** page 139)

The 1ST CANOEIST *to make a solo trip down the Mississippi* was Rebecca Johnson, a University of Iowa journalism student, who made the 2,400-mile run in 1974. Unimpressed with statistics showing that some two hundred people were defeated each summer before they could paddle to the first town, Johnson climbed into her canoe at Lake Itasca, Minnesota, on May 22 and headed south. Ninety-six days later, she arrived in New Orleans, Louisiana, having triumphed not only over the river but over the predictions of all the people who said she would not make it.

The 1ST CREW was introduced at Wellesley College in 1875. For eighteen years crew was considered less a competitive sport than a form of exercise and recreation. That was a fortunate approach in some ways, since the large, heavy craft then in use were almost impossible to maneuver and bore no resemblance to the sleek racing shells of today. Early boats at Wellesley were beamy enough to accommodate ten women dressed in long, billowing skirts. Eight sat amidships in pairs, handling the oars on either side, while two others, fore and aft, helped keep the boat on course. A secondary but equally important function of early crews was to row along the shore and serenade students and campus visitors. By the 1940s, women's crew had developed into a serious sport at Wellesley and other colleges, and in 1976, Joan Lund won a silver medal in single-shell rowing competition at the Montreal Olympics.

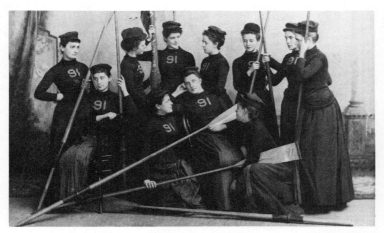

Pictured above are members of two of the early women's crew teams for Wellesley College, where the sport was first introduced in 1875. WELLESLEY COLLEGE

1ST DAREDEVIL *to conquer Niagara Falls in a barrel* was Annie Edson Taylor, a poor but ambitious schoolteacher from Bay City, Michigan, who at age forty-two concluded that she

Annie Edson Taylor stands beside a replica of the barrel that took her over Niagara Falls in 1901. Made of oak, it stood 4½ feet high and weighed 160 pounds. Most of the weight was from an anvil in the bottom, which kept the keg upright. Curiosity-seekers tore the original barrel to bits.
NIAGARA FALLS PUBLIC LIBRARY

could free herself from poverty only by doing something extraordinary, something no one else had ever done. Shortly thereafter, she designed a barrel and headed for the honeymoon city.

For a quarter of a century, daredevils of both sexes had been toppling over the lower, less treacherous rapids. One woman from Italy had even walked blindfolded across the river on a tightrope. But no man or woman had ever barreled over the great Horseshoe Falls and lived.

On October 24, 1901, Taylor's forty-third birthday, she crawled into her wooden keg, ordered the top bolted shut, and gave a muffled signal from within that she was ready to go. Thousands of onlookers lined the shores as her assistants set the leaky barrel free and its brave cargo bobbed and swirled toward the precipice. Then it plummeted over the crest of the falls and dropped 162 feet into the deadly whirlpools below. Harnesses designed to support her body inside the barrel failed and Taylor was slammed against the sides time after time. An hour later, rescuers snagged the keg downstream. They hurriedly sawed the top off, expecting to find her dead. Instead they found a soaked and barely conscious Annie Taylor, who gave a weak but triumphant wave. The crowd roared, churchbells rang, and newspapers rushed to press with the headlines "OVER THE FALLS AND STILL ALIVE! All Former Feats at Niagara Pale in Comparison ..." The accolades of that day were the greatest reward brave Annie was to gain, however. Souvenir-hunters tore her barrel to bits before she had even returned from receiving first aid. She built a replica in order to fulfill speaking and vaudeville engagements, but most of the money she had hoped to save ended up in her manager's pockets. Returning to Niagara Falls, she made a meager living selling autographed postcards to tourists. Penniless and almost blind, she died there on April 29, 1921. A public collection paid for her burial.

The **1ST GIRL SCOUTS** met on March 12, 1912, in the back yard of Juliette Gordon Low's home in Savannah, Georgia (see *First president of* the **GIRL SCOUTS,** page 141). Eight recruits from a local finishing school, who called themselves the White Rose Patrol after the state flower, and ten others known as the Carnation Patrol met there briefly to

Surrounded by an early troop of Girl Scouts, founder Juliette Gordon Low poses with the official "Be Prepared" banner in a Savannah back yard in 1913. By this time the original uniform had changed slightly and included a hat. GIRL SCOUTS OF AMERICA

call the roll. They then followed their leader, Page Wilder Anderson, next door to the home of a neighbor to have tea and plan their future. And what a future it was to be. Armed with their handbook *How Girls Can Help Their Country,* they would soon be enthusiastically engaged in all sorts of activities traditionally deemed inappropriate for young ladies. Besides showing them how to tie twelve useful knots, navigate by the stars, and build campfires, the book also schooled them on a wealth of more exotic forms of preparedness, such as "How to Stop a Runaway Horse" and "How to Secure a Burglar with Eight Inches of Cord." Their first uniform consisted of a dark blue middy blouse and skirt, and a light blue tie. Within two weeks of their historic first meeting, their ranks had doubled; and only two years later, their name now changed from Girl Guides to Girl

Scouts, their membership had grown to over a thousand. A troop of junior scouts, later to be known as Brownies, was organized in 1916.

1ST *president of the* **GIRL SCOUTS** was Juliette Gordon Low, born October 31, 1860, in Savannah, Georgia. Daisy, as she was called by family and friends, was properly educated in Savannah and New York but spent most of her young adulthood socializing and preparing herself for marriage. During one trip to Europe in 1884 she met Willie Low, a young English millionaire, whom she married a few years later. The Lows divided their time between their yacht and three different homes in Scotland, England, and America, entertaining heads of state, royalty, and various celebrities from the worlds of art and literature. Low died in 1901, and after a few years Daisy became concerned that her life had been wasted in useless frivolity. It was then that she encountered Sir Robert Baden-Powell, founder of the English Boy Scouts, and his sister, Agnes, who had just finished organizing the Girl Guides. Suddenly overcome by the importance of teaching young girls to actually be self-reliant and productive, she rushed back to Savannah determined to start a similar program. "I've got something for the girls of Savannah, and all of America, and all of the world," she exclaimed excitedly to a friend upon arrival, "and we're going to start it tonight!" After the first troops had been mustered in 1912 (see *First* **GIRL SCOUTS,** page 139), Low worked tirelessly to build the organization. Whenever the opportunity presented itself, she would captivate the girls with her repertoire of knot-tying and charm them with tales of her adventures in Paris, India, and Egypt. During World War I she sold her own pearls to finance the program through the wartime period. On January 17, 1927, only fifteen years after her dream had become a reality, Juliette Low died. By that time, her beloved Girl Scouts had become a nationwide organization with 150,000 members.

The **1ST** *black president of the* **GIRL SCOUTS** *was* thirty-seven-year-old Gloria D. Scott of Houston, Texas, who was elected in October 1975 for a three-year term. The third in a family of five children, Scott became involved in scouting at an early age. Later, after receiving her Ph.D. in higher education from Indiana University, she became active once again, joining the organization's national board in 1969 and being elected vice-president in 1972. As president, Scott helped initiate programs that would emphasize self-development over mere recreation, and in January 1977 she presided as the national board of directors endorsed the Equal Rights Amendment.

The **1ST** **HORSEBACK RIDER** *to make a coast-to-coast ride* was Nan Jane Aspinwall, who made the 3,000-mile trip in 301 days (108 actually spent traveling) just to show doubting friends that she could do it. Astride her bay mare, Lady Ellen, she galloped out of San Francisco on September 1, 1910. In her saddlebag was a letter from Mayor Patrick McCarthy of that city, to be delivered to Mayor William J. Gaynor of New York. The trip was not an easy one. Towns along the way were often less than friendly to Nan and her steed, who were sometimes forced to take shelter for the night in empty stalls or railroad stations. Though travel-weary, she nevertheless made a spectacular entrance into Manhattan on July 8, 1911. Dressed in a bright red shirt, divided skirt, and sombrero, she rode Lady Ellen right up to the steps of City Hall. The mayor, alas, was nowhere to be found, and an embarrassed aide accepted Mayor McCarthy's letter and welcomed Aspinwall to the city. After a few days of rest, horse and rider hit the trail again, this time for Atlantic City, New Jersey, where they were the star attractions of the 1911 Elks convention.

The **1ST JOCKEY** *to compete against men on a major U.S. flat track* was nineteen-year-old Diane Crump, who rode Merre Indian at Hialeah on February 7, 1969. In naming Crump to the mount, owner and trainer Mary Keim praised her ability, saying, "She's smart and I think she'll make as good a rider as any boy." The director of the Jockey's Guild, however, resented the encroachment of women onto the tracks. "Psychologically, a male jockey can't put his total concentration and best effort into a race when there's a female rider in there," he complained to the press. "He's too conscious of the woman's pres-

In 1970, Diane Crump became the first woman jockey to ride in the Kentucky Derby. She is pictured here before that race with her derby mount Fathom. WIDE WORLD

ence. Where is she? Is she in trouble? Is she going to do something foolish?" Crump rode a winner on only her sixth time out of the gate, and a year later, on May 2, 1970, she became the first female jockey to ride in the Kentucky Derby. Astride a colt named Fathom, a 10-to-1 shot, she finished fifteenth in a field of seventeen horses. (Another female jockey, Kathy Kusner, was licensed in 1968, before Crump, but did not race on a major track right away.)

The **1ST JOCKEY** *to win at a major U.S. flat track* was Barbara Jo Rubin, a nineteen-year-old former veterinary student who had learned to ride at Miami academies. She broke into thorough-bred racing as an exercise girl at Tropical Park, then earned her license early in 1969. Ready to ride, she was named to her first mount at that same track on January 15 of that year. However, male jockeys pelted her dressing room with rocks and threatened to leave the track if she rode, so officials pulled her from the ticket. Six weeks later, on February 22, she rode in— and won—her first race at Charles Town, Virginia, and within two months of that victory had finished first in half of twenty-two starts. Already tall at 5-foot-5 Rubin continued to grow. The extra height and weight, plus some serious medical complications resulting from knee injuries, forced her retirement only a little more than a year after her dazzling career had begun.

The **1ST MARATHON** *runner to win in open competition against men* was twenty-one-year-old Marion May of Fairbanks, Alaska. On June 14, 1975, she led a field of fifty-three male competitors in the Midnight Sun Marathon in Fairbanks, finishing first with a time of 3 hours, 2 minutes, and 41 seconds. It was the first time she had ever competed in a regulation marathon.

The **1ST** *unofficial Boston* **MARATHON** *competitor* was twenty-three-year-old Roberta Bengay. On the morning of the race in April 1966, she hid in the bushes near the starting line at Hopkinton, Massachusetts, and waited for the starter's gun to send the 416 men loping off toward Boston. Then she leapt from her hiding place and joined in behind them. Moving steadily up in the pack, Bengay crossed the finish line in 3 hours, 21 minutes, and 2 seconds, well ahead of two-thirds of the men. Embarrassed by her performance, marathon officials refused to even acknowledge her presence. "I know of no girl who ran in the Boston Marathon," said one. "I do know of a girl who is supposed to have run on the same roads as the marathon route today. But that's not the same."

The 1ST *"official"* Boston **MARATHON** *competitor* was Kathrine Switzer, a twenty-year-old member of the Syracuse University track team. Barred in 1967 from the prestigious long-distance race because of her sex, she mailed in her application under the name of K. Switzer, and on the day of the race asked a male runner to pick up her number. Buried in the middle of the pack and disguised in a hooded sweatsuit, she ran undetected for two miles until she threw back the hood and a news reporter yelled, "Number 261 is a broad!" A chase ensued as outraged officials tried unsuccessfully to remove her number. But Switzer kept running, and when she crossed the finish line into history some four hours and twenty-six miles later, she was promptly suspended from the Amateur Athletic Union for, among other things, running without a chaperone! The incident touched off a heated controversy in the United States

In 1967 a Boston Marathon official tries to throw Kathrine Switzer (No. 261) out of the race, which was then open only to men. Switzer, who had registered by mail and been issued a legitimate number, outran him and finished the race, becoming the first woman to "officially" do so. WIDE WORLD

that was not resolved until 1972 when officials finally backed down and allowed women to enter the Boston Marathon for the first time. Switzer, who went on to become a world-class marathon runner, won the women's title in the New York City Marathon in 1974 and finished first among American women at Boston in 1975, finishing second only to Liane Winter of West Germany.

The 1ST *officially sanctioned Boston* **MARATHON** *finisher* was thirty-three-year-old Nina Kuscik from Huntington, Long Island. After running unofficially for five years, women were finally permitted to enter the race in 1972, and on April 17 of that year Kuscik and eight other women competitors pinned on the first "F" (for female) numbers ever issued in the seventy-six-year history of this world-famous marathon. Leading the women, Kuscik crossed the finish line in 3 hours, 10 minutes, and 58 seconds, ahead of seven hundred (almost two-thirds) of the male runners. Finishing second among the women was Elaine Pederson of San Francisco, followed by Kathy Switzer of New York.

The 1ST MOTORCYCLISTS *to ride coast to coast* were Adeline Van Buren, 22, and her sister Augusta, 24, both from New York. Astride twin Indian motorcycles, they roared out of Sheepshead Bay in Brooklyn on July 4, 1916, bound for California. Their aim was to prove that should the United States become involved in World War I, women as well as men could be called upon to serve in the motorcycle corps. Traveling in identical leather jodhpurs, boots, jackets, and goggled helmets, the riders were repeatedly arrested in one tiny town after another for "wearing men's clothes" but always released on the condition that they leave town at once. With 5,500 dusty miles behind them, they rolled to a stop in Hollywood, California, on September 2, sixty days after their departure. They had detoured once along the way to ride up Pikes Peak on their bikes, becoming the first women to scale that mountain on any kind of motorized vehicle.

After a routine service stop at an Omaha bike shop, Adeline and Augusta Van Buren prepare to hit the road again on their transcontinental ride. ANNE TULLY RUDERMAN

The 1ST MOUNTAINCLIMBER *to scale Mount Rainier* was twenty-year-old Fay Fuller, who reached the top of the 14,410-foot mountain, the third highest in the nation, on August 10, 1890.

Without the benefit of modern climbing attire or special equipment, Fay Fuller scrambled to the top of Mount Rainier in 1890. WASHINGTON STATE HISTORICAL SOCIETY

She wore wool gloves and a heavy pair of boy's shoes, and under her long dress, several layers of underclothing and bloomers. For equipment, she relied only upon a blanket roll, which she kept tied securely over one shoulder during the climb, and a homemade alpenstock fashioned from a shovel handle.

The **1ST MOUNTAINCLIMBERS** *to scale Mt. Annapurna* were Irene Miller, 43, from Palo Alto, California, and Vera Komarkova, 35, from Boulder, Colorado, members of a ten-woman team organized by Arlene Blum, a California biochemist. The women flew to Nepal on August 6, 1978, and from there walked eighty miles to the foot of the mountain. On August 26, accompanied by six Sherpa guides (two of whom were women), the team began the climb. On October 15, Miller and Komarkova reached the 26,545-foot pinnacle, the first women and the first Americans to do so. The expedition was marred by the deaths of two team members, Alison Chadwick-Onszkiewicz and Vera Watson, who fell at the 24,000-foot level on October 18. The other members of the team were Joan Firey, Liz Klobusicky, Piro Kramar, Margi Rusmore, and Anne Whitehouse. Only one team of British men had previously scaled the main peak, although three other groups had conquered the lower ones, including a team of two Japanese women who reached Annapurna III (24,000 feet) in 1970.

1ST OLYMPIC GOLD MEDALIST was Margaret Abbott, who won the Women's International Golf Match in Paris in 1900. The match was an Olympic event, but Abbott's title was considered unofficial because women had not yet been sanctioned to compete in the Olympics. In 1920, Ethelda Bleibtrey became the first American woman to hold an official Olympic title, for swimming, which had been introduced as an event in 1912. Shortly thereafter, in that same Olympics, another American woman, Aileen Riggins, won a gold medal for springboard diving. (The first event officially sanctioned for women was figure skating, but the title did not go to an American until 1956, when seventeen-year-old Tenley Albright won the gold medal.)

1ST *runner to win three* **OLYMPIC GOLD MEDALS** was Wilma Rudolph. Born June 23, 1940, in St. Bethlehem, Tennessee, she suffered attacks of double pneumonia and scarlet fever as a young child and could not even walk without braces until she was eleven years old. Determined to overcome her disability, she exercised diligently and learned to play basketball in her back yard. By the time she went to high school she was a champion athlete, breaking records in track as well as basketball. Adding world records as a Tennessee State University sprinter the nineteen-year-old began to set her sights on the Olympics. In the summer of 1960 in Rome, she sprinted to three Olympic victories to take home gold medals for the 100-meter dash, the 200-meter dash (an Olympic record), and the 400-meter relay (a world record).

1ST PARACHUTIST *to jump from an airplane* was Georgia "Tiny" Thompson Broadwick. A crowd-pleaser at air shows and carnivals from the age of fifteen, Tiny specialized in leaping out of hot-air balloons at an altitude of 1,000–2,000 feet and miraculously descending to the ground under three successively released parachutes of red, white, and blue. For performing this death-defying feat six times a week she was paid a whopping $250 by aerial inventor Charles Broadwick, whose last name she adopted as did all the members of his exhibition team. In Los Angeles, California, on June 21, 1913, Tiny became the first woman in the world to make a parachute jump from an airplane. Perched on a platform suspended under the plane's right wing, she waited until pilot Glenn Martin brought the craft to within jumping distance of Griffith Park. Then she tripped a lever that released her trap seat, floated smoothly through the air, and made a stylish stand-up landing to the cheers of a waiting crowd. One year later the U.S. Army became interested in outfitting pilots with self-contained pack-type chutes and commissioned Tiny Broadwick to test the new equipment before the Army Aviation Bureau at Rockwell Field in San Diego. On

Swinging precariously under the plane's wing, parachutist Georgia "Tiny" Thompson Broadwick prepares to make her first jump.
NATIONAL AIR AND SPACE MUSEUM, SMITHSONIAN INSTITUTION

September 13 she made four successive jumps, leaving the rip cord connected to the aircraft in the conventional manner. Just prior to the fifth and last jump, the cord became tangled, so Tiny cut it loose and held onto the ends herself. Then she dove out and plummeted head first toward the earth in the first premeditated free-fall jump by any person. She opened the chute manually on the way down and made a perfect landing at the feet of an astonished General George P. Scriver. The general was so impressed that he promptly placed the Army's first order for parachutes. Tiny stopped jumping in 1922 but remained active in the field of aviation until she retired at age seventy-two.

Karren Stead, her left arm in a cast from an accident incurred the previous day, drove her racer to victory in the National Soap Box Derby at Akron, Ohio, in 1975. She collected the first championship title ever won by a female—and a $3,000 scholarship.
ALL-AMERICAN SOAP BOX DERBY

The 1ST SOAP BOX DERBY CHAMPION was eleven-year-old Karren Stead of Morrisville, Pennsylvania, who won the title on August 3, 1975. Driving a sleek, low-slung fiberglass racer that she designed and built herself, Karren had qualified for the nationals by winning a regional race the month before. Then both driver and car went to Akron, Ohio, for the thirty-eighth running of the famous downhill derby, known as the Indy of the soap box set. In a series of prefinal heats, Stead eliminated all but two competitors, both boys. Then, with her ninety-five-pound frame tucked all the way into the racer so that only the top of her helmet showed, she breezed down the 950-foot sloping track in 27.52 seconds to collect the championship and a $3,000 scholarship.

The 1ST professional **SOFTBALL** *league* was formed in 1976 by Billie Jean King and a group of sports entrepreneurs. Called the International Women's Professional Softball Association (IWPSA), the league offered investors a ten-team breakdown divided evenly between Eastern and Western cities. King herself made the first team purchase in partnership with golfer Jane Blalock and tennis pro Martina Navratalova. They bought the Connecticut Falcons, headed by amateur champion Joan Joyce, world famous for terrifying batters with her 110-mph pitches, who was also a co-owner. The league began its first season on May 28 of that year and finished in September with a world series between the San Jose Sunbirds of the Western Division and the Eastern Division Falcons. The Falcons swept the series in four games.

The 1ST **STEAMBOAT CAPTAIN** *on the Mississippi* was Mary Becker Greene. Born in 1869 near Marietta, Ohio, she married riverboat captain Gordon C. Greene and learned how to steer paddlewheelers on her honeymoon. Within a few years she was skilled enough to obtain both her pilot's and master's licenses, so when the Greenes acquired a second boat in 1894, Captain Mary Greene took charge of it. For the next eighteen years she cargoed whiskey, soap, paint, and other items up and down the Mississippi, bearing three sons on board along the way. The third child arrived as her boat, the *Argand*, was stuck in an ice jam. When her husband died in 1927,

Captain Mary Greene piloted steamboats on the Mississippi for forty years and eventually owned eleven of the giant paddlewheelers. One of them, the *Delta Queen* (shown above), is piloted by a woman today. FREDERICK WAY, JR. DELTA QUEEN STEAMBOAT COMPANY

"Ma" Greene, as she had come to be known by the crew, assumed the management of the company, which by then boasted a fleet of eleven sternwheelers. She took the helm of the largest one, named the *Gordon C. Greene* after her late husband, and held the operation together through the Depression, when most of the other steamer companies folded. In 1935 she reopened passenger service on the Mississippi, a mode of transportation unavailable since the Civil War. Mary Greene retired as a full-time steamboat captain in 1937 but continued to occupy quarters aboard the *Gordon C. Greene* for almost ten years until she moved to a stateroom on the company's recently acquired packet, the *Delta Queen*. She died there on April 22, 1949, at the age of eighty. Both the *Delta Queen* and the company Captain Mary Greene helped found (now called the Delta Queen Steamboat Company) are still in operation today.

The 1ST STEAMBOAT CAPTAIN *west of the Mississippi* was Minnie Hill of Portland, Oregon, who obtained her riverboat captain's license (both pilot's and master's tickets) in 1886. Her boat, a steamboat packet called the *Governor Newell,* made regular runs along the Columbia River for many years with Captain Hill at the helm.

The 1ST STEAMBOAT CAPTAIN *of the Delta Queen* was Lexie Palmore, 30, of Tyler, Texas, who received her license to pilot the classic 285-foot passenger steamboat on November 18, 1978. Shortly thereafter, she reported aboard at Cincinnati, Ohio, as one of the three operators simultaneously required by the giant paddlewheeler. Captain Palmore, an artist with a master's degree, began her career on the *Delta Queen* as a chambermaid. After working one summer on the boat, she decided to go back to school, this time to the National River Academy in Helena, Arkansas, to learn how to operate large riverboats. Sponsored at the maritime school by the Delta Queen Steamboat Company, Palmore was its first female student. She completed the two-year course at the head of her class, and scored an average of 97.7 percent on her Coast Guard licensing exams (see *First female* **STEAMBOAT CAPTAIN** *on the Mississippi*, page 155).

1ST SULLIVAN AWARD *winner* was swimmer Ann Curtis, who won in 1944. The award, named for James Sullivan, former president of the Amateur Athletic Union, was first given in 1930. It is awarded to the amateur athlete whose performance, example, and influence have done the most during that year to advance the cause of sportsmanship. It would be twelve more years before another woman, this time diving champ Pat McCormack, would win the award.

1ST SWIMMER *to cross the English Channel* was Gertrude ("Trudy") Ederle, who plunged into the stormy water at Cap Gris-Nez, France, on August 6, 1926. She had struggled only halfway across the frigid channel when her manager begged her to quit. Ederle refused, and when she touched the beach at Dover, England, 14 hours and 35 minutes later, the first woman ever to make the crossing, she had swum the distance two hours faster than the fastest man. Ederle became an instant heroine and remained highly popular as a public figure until a back injury and partial loss of hearing brought her professional career to an end. She continued to use her athletic skills, however, teaching deaf children to swim.

The **1ST SWIMMER** *to cross the English Channel in both directions* was Florence Chadwick, a thirty-two-year-old Californian who financed her swimming career by working as a stenographer. On August 8, 1950, she broke the record for the France-to-England swim, which had been held since 1926 by Gertrude Ederle, the first woman to cross the channel. However, no woman, and only nine men, had successfully challenged it from the other direction. On September 11, 1951, she waded into the whitecapped channel at Dover, England, and after 16 hours and 22 minutes in the chilling water, dragged herself ashore at Calais, France. Two years later she made the same swim two hours faster.

The **1ST SWIMMER** *to break the record for circling the island of Manhattan* was twenty-six-year-old Diana Nyad, a veteran marathoner. Among her previous swims were those across Lake Ontario and the Nile River. On October 7, 1975, Nyad slipped into New York's East River and headed upstream at a powerful sixty strokes per minute. Eleven days earlier, she had been dragged from the water, exhausted, in a first, unsuccessful attempt to circum-

Diana Nyad nears the end of her 1975 marathon swim around Manhattan. CARY HERZ

navigate the city. This time, however, she overcame the cold water temperature, strong currents, and pollution to complete the twenty-eight-mile loop in 7 hours and 57 minutes. Her time was faster by nearly an hour than the existing record, held for forty-eight years by a man. (The first woman ever to make the swim was Ida Elionsky, who circled the city on September 5, 1916, in 11 hours and 35 minutes. In 1959 Diane Struble made the swim 14 minutes faster than Elionsky.) In 1979, Nyad announced that she would swim from the Bahamas to the U.S. mainland, a sixty-mile stretch of the Atlantic Ocean never crossed by any swimmer. On her first attempt, August 4, she was stopped only twelve miles out by stinging jellyfish that left her nearly paralyzed. A fortnight later, however, she plunged into the surf at Bimini once again. Gulf Stream currents pulled her so far off course that when she triumphantly waded ashore at Jupiter, Florida, 27 hours and 38 minutes later, she had swum 89 miles.

The 1ST UMPIRE *in professional baseball* was forty-one-year-old Berenice Gera from New York City. After a five-year struggle for acceptance by organized baseball, Gera had to sue before landing an umpire's contract in the Class A New York–Penn (minor) League in January 1972. She called her first game between Geneva and Auburn in Geneva, New York, on June 25 of that year. Unfortunately, it was also her last. Deeply resented, she had been the target of threats and criticism for weeks, and when a miscalled play brought even further abuse from the Auburn team manager, Gera called it quits. Later she told reporters, "They succeeded in getting rid of me ... but I succeeded, too. I've broken the barrier. It can be done." Gera did not totally retire from baseball; she moved to a job in the Mets front office.

The 1ST VARSITY *letter winner at a military academy* was Cadet Susan K. Donner of Longmeadow, Massachusetts. A member of the first class at the U.S. Coast Guard Academy to which women were admitted, the eighteen-year-old Donner won her letter in November 1976 for outstanding skill as both skipper and crew in intercollegiate sailing competition. (In March 1977, Midshipman Peggy Feldman of San Antonio, Texas, became the first woman to win a varsity letter from the U.S. Naval Academy. She was a swimmer.)

The 1ST *member of a male college* **VARSITY TEAM** was Sally Brown, a senior at Rollins College in Winter Park, Florida. Because of her diminutive size, Brown was recruited as the coxswain of the 1936 Rollins shell. She trained with the crew, then led them in their only two races of the season, in May and June. Although women's rowing had been introduced at Wellesley College in 1893 (see *First women's* **CREW,** page 136), it didn't become a serious sport for college women until the late 1940s.

Seated at the far right end of a column of oarsmen is Sally Brown, coxswain of the 1936 Rollins College shell. Inset photo is her yearbook picture. ROLLINS COLLEGE

AFTERWORD

The following individuals, institutions, and organizations were helpful in providing information and material for this book: the Air Force Museum, Denver, Colorado; Sr. Alberta, The American Sisters of Charity; American Telephone and Telegraph; Russell Barnes, the Delta Queen Steamboat Company; Ursula Beach, the Montgomery County, Tennessee, Historical Society; the Margaret Clapp Library, Wellesley College; Helen Collins, *Naval Aviation News;* Sr. Columba, The Ursaline Academy at New Orleans; Brenda Dill, *The St. Petersburg Times;* Melba Ferguson, the Girl Scouts of America; Frontier Airlines; Ronda Goldstein, United Airlines; Jeff Iula, the All-American Soap Box Derby; Donald Lokur, the Niagara Falls Public Library; Jim Loveland, the Southern Pacific Transportation Company; Pauline Moody, the Sharon, Massachusetts, Historical Society; the Museum of the American Indian, New York; Ruth McCandliss, the Miss America Pageant; Robert McLeod, the Lowell, Massachusetts, Public Library; the Ninety-Nines, Inc.; the National Aeronautical Association; the National Air and Space Museum of the Smithsonian Institution; the New York Public Library Picture Collection; Lexie Alvarez and Stephanie Hosie, Rollins College; Pattie J. Scott, the Richmond, Virginia Public Library; the Scripps-Howard Broadcasting Company; the Sophia Smith Collection, Smith College; the Schlesinger Library, Radcliffe College; Evelyn Summers, the Fayette County, Tennessee,

Historical Society; the U.S. Air Force Academy; the U.S. Coast Guard Academy; the U.S. Coast Guard Officer Candidate School, Yorktown, Virginia; the U.S. Naval Academy; the U.S. Military Academy; Vassar College Library; the Washington State Historical Society; Lela Wimp, the Argonia, Kansas, Historical Society.

INDEX

Note: Page numbers in boldface indicate illustrations